Nothing is Certain, and the Dead Walk

Shawn McLain

Nothing Is Certain, and the Dead Walk

Copyright © 2010 by Shawn McLain

ISBN: 978-1-7329408-2-6

Nothing is Certain, and the Dead Walk

SHAWN MCLAIN

A Good Time Spoiled

The wait had been twenty minutes for a seat on a busy Friday night. The restaurant was not a fancy one but more of a casual dining experience. But for the seventeen-year-old boy who was paying for this date, it was rather extravagant. Tim Powers and Nikki McLaren had been dating for a year now, and this was their special anniversary dinner.

Tim's smile was strained as he tried not to think about the few bills he had in his wallet. The waitress frowned as she handed them their menus and took drink orders. She knew a decent tip was not likely. Nikki glanced over the menu, noting Tim's discomfort. She knew he wanted this to be special, but she also knew he didn't really have much money. Trying to pick out the least expensive item on the menu turned out to be some pasta or a sandwich. She decided on a sandwich, as there was less likelihood of getting sauce on her shirt that way. She had taken more time than usual to look good for tonight and wasn't about to ruin it with red sauce.

Smiling, she began to look around. The walls were covered with movie and sports memorabilia. There was a bar in the middle of the restaurant that was on a lower level than the rest of the dining area. Their table was right next to the rail overlooking the bar. She wondered why they called it a bar when more people sat eating at it than drinking.

"More like a lunch counter," she mumbled.

"What was that?" Tim asked nervously.

"Nothing, just looking around." She smiled. Further conversation was interrupted by the waitress taking their order.

As Tim debated his meal, Nikki returned to her observations. She noticed several families eating at the larger tables. There was what looked like a birthday party for a five-year-old where several young girls were making a lot of noise while a very pale, tired-looking woman tried to keep them in control. Her husband was doing what he could to help while constantly whispering to her. The woman would give a weak smile and wave off his concerns.

Nikki watched the family until Tim recalled her attention by finally making a decision. With the ordering out of the way, Nikki gave her full attention back to her boyfriend. As they began to talk, she forgot about the other people around them. They talked about school and where they wanted to go to college. Tim was hinting about living arrangements after graduation, but Nikki breezed over it. She really liked Tim, maybe even loved him, but she was young and not ready for that kind of commitment.

She noticed the disappointment in Tim's eyes, but he rallied quickly. He cast around for things to say until he noticed a drunk at the bar. The man was slumped over, and the bartender was shaking him by the shoulder, trying to talk to him. The drunk would move his head and shoulders barely off the bar. Nikki watched as the bartender leaned in close. The drunk seemed to be trying to talk to him.

"Wow! That dude is seriously hammered!" Tim laughed.

Nikki looked over again. She cringed as the drunk was being urged to his feet by a middle-aged waitress and someone who appeared to be the manager. "I just hope he doesn't...*ooooohhhhhh!*" Nikki cried and covered her eyes as the man began to throw up on the waitress's shoes. She cried out, letting the man go in disgust. He crumpled to the floor, apparently unconscious. Several people were now craning their necks to see what was going on. The manager was angrily whispering to the bartender as another waitress hovered over the downed man.

Nikki felt bad for the birthday party, thinking the young girl would be upset. She glanced across the bar to the party table. No one there seemed to notice what was going on. Nikki gasped as she watched the harried mother fall over, convulsing. "Oh my God!" she exclaimed while rising to her feet and pointing at the woman.

Tim turned in his seat to see what she was pointing at. Several patrons had rushed to help in both areas. Tim was watching the bar when, without warning, the drunk stood up. He swayed for a moment and then lunged at the waitress who was trying to steady him. She screamed as he bit into her shoulder.

"Oh, here we go—a fight!" Tim exclaimed grumpily. "Maybe we should…"

The bartender had jumped over the bar to help the waitress. He screamed as the drunk bit hard into his arm. Blood blossomed over his white dress shirt. A man jumped forward and grabbed the drunk around the neck, pulling him off the bleeding man. Next moment, the Good Samaritan was also screaming in agony as he, too, was bitten. Blood poured from a wound on his cheek.

"Oh God! He's chewing on it!" Tim cried, jumping to his feet.

Screams erupted across the room. Everywhere Nikki looked, she saw panic. She was watching through a tunnel as her attention focused on the birthday party. Everything around her seemed to go into slow motion. The woman who had fallen ill was now in a seated position on the floor. She was holding the arm of a struggling little girl and chewing on the little girl's severed fingers, letting the bones fall from her mouth as the young girl screamed. The woman's husband was trying desperately to pull the girl free as the other children ran in terror. Time seemed to go from slow motion to regular to fast-forward as Nikki took in the entire scene.

The bartender lay on the floor, a pool of blood spreading around his fallen body. Several people had now run for the door. Nikki watched, frozen in her place. Another woman was now pulling on the little girl, trying to help; this went unnoticed by the one happily munching on the little girl's hand. The man heaved, and the little girl flew to him. Blood sprayed across a *Dracula* poster from the empty shoulder, her arm still back with the blood-soaked woman on the floor. The waitress, shirt covered in her own blood, turned, with ragged flesh hanging from her mouth as she searched for the meal that was taken from her. The girl's screams were drowned out by all those screaming around her. The man tried to stem the flow that kept spraying from the torn shoulder. The feasting woman looked down at the severed limb. A look of anger crossed her face, and she dropped it. The little girl went limp in the man's arms. The woman was on her feet, grabbing at the people running past her. The bartender was now on his feet. Blood dripped down his chin as he bit into the waitress with vomit on her shoes.

Chaos reigned. The exit door was now crammed with people trying to escape. Tables crashed to the ground, sending plates, glasses, and food clattering to the floor. Chairs that were flung aside by fleeing patrons tripped up those scrambling for the exits. Nikki's chair collided with her knees, sending her crashing painfully into the table as the large woman behind her jumped to her feet. Hands grabbed her, pulling her off the table. Nikki screamed in terror and pain as her legs became tangled in her fallen chair. She felt as if her own arm was being torn off by a large man with a wild beard. As she regained her feet, the burly man yelled something and thrust her into another set of arms. She calmed slightly at seeing Tim. He was holding her roughly around the waist, pushing her with the rest of the crowd toward the exit. All breath was forced from her when the bearded man yanked both her and Tim back. The bartender, the waitress, the drunk, and many others were now attacking the plug of people at the exit.

A window shattered behind them. Tim's grip failed him, as the huge arms were around Nikki again. She was pushed along with the throng toward the newly opened escape portal. She craned her neck and saw what looked like Tim running across the bar toward the takeout-order door. The woman from the party lunged at him, but Nikki couldn't see what happened next. She was off her feet. The beard was in her eyes as the man picked her up and threw her out the window, a thorny bush cushioning her fall. His huge feet landed on the ground next to her, and he grabbed her arm and pulled her away from the building just in time to avoid being trampled by the flood of bodies scrambling out.

"No! No! No! I have to find my boyfriend!" Nikki screamed, tugging her arm free of her savior.

"Come on, girl, we have to get out of here!" exclaimed the huge man. Blood ran down his arm from a long gash. He stutter-stepped, backing up.

"I have to find Tim!" she cried.

The man held out his hands, gave her an imploring look, and then ran off to the parking lot. Tires squealed and screams rang as Nikki stood on the sidewalk being jostled as people ran by. Finally, she ran toward where Tim had parked.

A man was running across the lot as a truck barreled around the corner. It slammed into the man, sending him flying through the air. Nikki watched, transfixed, as the man gracefully arced through the air, his arms and legs out like a huge jack, spinning end over end. Then, with a horrid crunch audible over the screams, he hit the ground. Nikki stood staring as the sight sank in. The truck hadn't even slowed. Slowly there was a twitch. The man raised his head and half of his body. The other half turned at an impossible angle, stayed still on the bloody pavement. He reached out a hand with broken fingers toward her. His bloody face held no sign of distress. The hand he held out was not pleading for help. His mouth opened, showing broken, red-stained teeth. His eyes wanted her; this man wanted to kill her. She felt it in her soul as she stared back into those blank, hungry eyes.

That was all it took; she was running now. Sounds were assaulting her ears. Sirens blared, tires screeched, and people screamed. Several times she staggered as someone ran into her, and once she was knocked into the street. She had nearly been killed by a minivan that ended up embedded in a storefront. Nikki was several blocks from the restaurant now. She cowered in a doorway, trying to ascertain where she was. She recognized the street. That was the coffee shop where she would go with Tim, and there was the crappy theater no one ever went to. She was in Glendale, not far from the school. She knew where to go: one street over. She ran down an alley and across the road to the Stop-In Mart convenience store. The lights were on! Nikki ran to the door. Yanking it open, she ducked inside. Her friend Tonya was behind the counter.

"Nikki! What the hell is going on? My parents keep calling me to come home," Tonya demanded when Nikki slammed through the door. "And what the hell happened to you?"

The fluorescent lights dazzled her eyes. Bending over to catch her breath, Nikki could see that the hard work she had put into getting ready for the anniversary dinner had been demolished. Her shirt was damp with sweat; what had been a pretty light blue was now filthy with blood and dirt. She wasn't sure if it was hers or from the man who saved her. She felt guilty for not thanking him. The dirt was from the bushes and the several times she had been knocked to the ground. Her jeans, torn and stained, and her knees, bruised and bloodied, bore witness to that fact.

Tonya had come out from behind the counter and was holding Nikki by the shoulders. "What the hell is going on? The radio is saying riots or something," Tonya demanded, shaking Nikki slightly. Suddenly Tonya looked around behind Nikki. "Where is Tim?" she whispered.

"I don't know," Nikki said, choking up. "We got separated." Nikki then told Tonya everything that had happened.

Both girls jumped as Tonya's phone rang. She answered and listened. Nikki could hear Tonya's father order her home. Nikki rummaged through her pockets but couldn't find her own phone.

"I gotta go home," Tonya explained.

"Can I get a ride?" Nikki asked hopefully.

Pink crept up into Tonya's cheeks. "I'm on my bike. I...I got caught speeding, and Dad took the car privilege away."

The phone rang again. Tonya listened for a second and then ran over to the counter. She flipped a couple of switches, plunging the store into darkness except for an emergency light near the back. Nikki heard keys jingling as Tonya hurried to the front. The light from Tonya's phone went out. "That was my manager; he said to get out and lock up." Tonya waited at the door.

Nikki looked at her. "Can I borrow your phone?" she asked while holding out her hand. Tonya looked at the phone and then outside.

"I really need to go," Tonya whispered.

"I'll get it back to you tomorrow. I promise," Nikki said, her hand still outstretched.

"Come on," Tonya replied while opening the door. "I need to lock up."

"I can do that, lock up. Please, I don't want to be out there walking around."

Tonya looked from Nikki's outstretched hand to her own bike and then back. Keys and phone in hand, Nikki turned the lock and watched her friend ride off. The phone rang, and Nikki answered.

"Tonya, where the hell are you?" Tonya's father's voice boomed through the speaker. "Your mother says the police won't let her downtown."

"She's on her way home, Mr. Van Wert," Nikki assured him.

"Nikki? Is that you? Where are you? Why do you have Tonya's phone? Is she OK?"

Nikki told the story again to her friend's father. It was harder now as she heard more sirens and what she assumed was gunfire. He listened carefully, telling her to call her parents.

"Let me know the minute someone comes to get you. If I haven't heard from you in an hour, we will come to get you," he assured her.

Nikki thanked Mr. Van Wert. She crouched behind the counter, trying to decide her next move. A loud thud against the storefront and a bloody streak across the glass made a decision for her. Nikki crept to the back of the dark, empty store. She dialed her home number, and it rang and rang. She sat and racked her brain, trying to remember Tim's number. He was always in her contacts list; she never dialed it. She tried several numbers. Finally, after several wrong numbers and being screamed at for not being a loved one the person on the other end needed to talk to, she got his voice mail. She begged him to call as soon as possible. She then tried her family again; no answer. She tried Tonya's family; no answer. She then couldn't make any calls, as "all the circuits are full," according to the voice in the phone.

The hour came and went, and no one came. Then it was two hours. Several people ran by the store, but no one was looking for her. The sun rose to find her still staring out the front window, waiting for someone to help her.

Worst Day Ever

"Where is this place?" Ray demanded of his wife.

"Turn left at the church; then go down a block and then take a right, and it should be the fourth one down," Krissy informed her father from the back seat.

"How did you…oh," he began and then stopped as she held up her iPhone.

His wife just stared out the window. He placed a hand on her arm. "He knows where we are going. He'll be OK," Ray told Jennifer.

They passed a burning building and a wrecked car. Ray slammed on the brakes, swerving as several people ran out in front of the car. From the back seat, Krissy whimpered and ducked down, not watching as the car passed the group. Voices shouted unintelligible noise at them.

"It's OK, sweetie. They were OK." Jen turned to reassure her daughter.

"Oh shit!" The car slowed.

"Ray!" Jen hissed. Ray returned her admonishment with a quick shake of the head.

"Krissy, honey, find your dad another way to Uncle Alistair's place. Just look at your phone, OK?" Jen looked from her husband to the road in front of them. It was blocked. Their way was completely blocked by people slowly moving forward. It was them, the not-OK ones.

Ray eased the car to a stop, trying to be as calm as possible. His heart pounded painfully against his ribs. He was aware that Krissy was beginning to panic in the back seat, and Jen was clutching the dashboard, white-knuckled. He put the car in reverse and began to turn around as quickly as he could, his foot jamming on the brake. A large truck barreled past them.

Jen watched it as it smashed into the crowd that was blocking the road.

"Follow him, follow him, *follow* while we can!" she screamed to her husband. Ray straightened the car out and sped into the other vehicle's wake.

"Close your eyes, Krissy—do it now!" Ray yelled at his daughter. She closed her eyes tight as the tears ran down her face. Hands hit the windows, and legs cracked under the wheels. Jen clutched the seat belt, willing the car forward. Ray held out as long as he could. The horde began to close in, and he let out a scream as they plowed through. Red splotches appeared on the hood and the windshield, and blood and hair stuck in the spider-web crack in the glass. Ray cried out in victory as the street opened up before him. Trembling hands clutching the wheel, he sped down the open road, barely slowing to take the turn by the church.

"Kyle is gonna meet us, right?" Krissy begged from behind her mother, breaking the woman's heart just a little more. She had no idea where her son was or how to tell her daughter that.

Best Day Ever

"This is the best day ever!" Kyle shouted, pounding the ceiling of the car in jubilation. The tires squealed as he took a corner. A woman screamed as he came within inches of her. "Yeah, whatever!" he shouted out the window. His hand found the dash and clicked on the radio. He tried channel after channel before giving up with a disgusted grunt.

"Shut up! Fucking boring-ass news," he grumbled and reached into the CD carrier next to him. Pulling the album to him, he flipped through the disks. "Crap, crap, double crap. Seriously? Who bought this shit?" he demanded of the interior while throwing the offending disks out the window.

"Sweet! Ozzy!" Sliding the disk into the player, he cranked up "Crazy Train" and reached for the handgun on the passenger seat. He slowed as he came to another corner. A man stood there, staring at him. His mouth hung open and slack. They stared at each other for several seconds. The man groaned while he reached out for him. Kyle smiled and pointed the gun at the man. He pulled the trigger, and the weapon jumped in his hand as the man's head exploded into a crimson spray. The body crumpled to the ground. Kyle pumped his fist.

"Yes! Ten more points. Best day ever!" he shouted and grabbed a beer from the back seat. Popping the top of the bottle, he took a long, deep drink. He looked into the rearview mirror. A crowd was starting to descend on him.

"Time to go." He grunted as he finished the beer in one last gulp. Putting the car in gear, he flung the empty bottle out the window. It hit a little girl who was coming up quickly to the car. Kyle laughed, giving the girl the finger.

A police car screamed past him; he just gave it a wave as he headed through the streets. Pounding the dashboard along to the beat, he pushed the accelerator to the floor. Backing off the gas, Kyle fumbled behind him for another beer. Tires squealed as a sedan whipped around the corner, coming up fast on him. "Go around, dickhead," Kyle grumbled, still fishing for a drink. The sedan was right on him. He could see the driver and passenger gesturing to each other and pointing at him. "Yo, asshole!" Kyle yelled, waving the gun, being sure they could see it. He frowned as the couple in the front seat high-fived. The woman in the passenger seat was bracing herself. The driver held an evil grin.

The impact sent Kyle's gun to the floor, clattering among several empty bottles. He could see the woman laughing, pulling a shotgun out from the back seat. Kyle swerved when the woman hung out of the window and fired. The shots missed! Kyle swerved into the oncoming lane. Smoke billowed from the tires. Kyle's feet were on the brake, his back sunk into the seat with the pressure. The sedan sped past. He looked left and then right—no way out. Not enough room to turn around without getting shot. He decided to make a break for the road ahead. The street ended in a T junction. Standing on the gas, he knew he would have to take the turn at the last second.

"Yeah, that's right, I have a gun!" he screamed, firing two shots out of the window, coming up fast on the other car. He wasn't aiming; he just didn't want them to fire back. He laughed as the couple ducked down. The smile faded from his face as the passenger leveled the shotgun and fired. Kyle jerked the wheel when he saw the gun. The rear window of the sedan in front of him exploded. The passenger side of the front window spider-webbed as buckshot shredded the passenger-seat headrest.

"Motherfucker! It's so on now, bitch!" Kyle screamed at the vehicle in front of him. Leaning his head out of the window, he fired at the woman. The driver swerved, throwing her left and right as she tried to shoot back at Kyle. She fired, pellets peppering the front of the car and roof. Kyle cried out in pain and frustration as his arm was hit. He fired at the driver. The car lurched to the left, hit two parked cars, and then slammed into the building at the junction. Kyle slammed on the brakes, stopping several feet behind the wrecked car. "Oh shit, oh shit, oh shit," Kyle breathed.

Relief and terror fought for control as the passenger door creaked open and the woman stumbled out, trailing several gold chains. Kyle could see boxes of electronics in the back seat. The woman was raising the shotgun. Kyle gunned the engine and slammed into the woman. She bounced off the hood and flew into the crumbling bricks of the building they had just hit.

Tears were in the corner of his eyes. "Yeah! How 'bout that? Huh? Had to fucking shoot at me. Now you were worth twenty points for being a stupid bitch!" Kyle was panting, tears running down his cheeks. "All I was doing was trying to scare you, stupid!" He put the car into reverse as the driver of the wrecked car pushed the door open and stumbled out. The woman slowly got up and joined the man as they came after the car. She fell behind, dragging a broken leg, and her arm swung uselessly at her side.

Swiping angrily at his wet face, Kyle shouted at them, "You just had to leave me alone, that's all. Well, that's what happens now. Nobody is gonna fuck with *me*! *This is the best day ever!*"

Watching

Alistair sat in the huge den, watching the sixty-inch LCD screen. Images flashed across the display. Amid the screams and scenes of panic, the newscaster spoke. The forced-calm voice talked of scientific research, governments set up in safe locations, and military efforts. Information scrolled along the bottom of the screen constantly. The information was about evacuation points and safety precautions.

"Really falling apart out there," Alistair's wife Rebecca noted as she descended the three steps into the den.

"Yeah, have you heard from Jen and Ray yet?" he asked.

"They were heading to the house when we got cut off," she responded, pacing the room. Alistair picked up the remote and changed the channel from a screaming reporter and the blurred scene to a quiet, still courtyard of a large house. He picked up another remote, and the picture changed to another camera with a shot of a wall and a road. Several people were wandering along the road.

"Damn, are they close to the gate?" Rebecca asked. Alistair reached over to a panel that had several buttons and two small joysticks on it. He selected a button and then moved the joysticks. The camera panned down the road.

"Plenty of time, if they don't mess up the code too many times," Alistair replied, an edge to his voice. As if on cue, a Volvo pulled up to the main gate.

"They're there!" Rebecca breathed and gripped the back of the couch. Alistair moved to the edge of the seat, watching the big screen. He selected the camera for the front gate.

"Come on, Ray, come on," he urged. A small alarm began to beep on the control panel next to him. "He's messed it up." Alistair shook his head. The people in the streets were moving toward the car. The alarm beeped again.

"Why didn't we put in an opener here?" Rebecca demanded of the couch. Alistair didn't answer. The contractor had made the same suggestion, but Alistair had decided to save the money. "It's not like we couldn't afford it," she continued anxiously. Alistair groaned internally. He hated when she was right.

The alarm beeped again. "Damn it, Ray! Get it together!" Alistair yelled. Suddenly the alarm turned from red to green. The couple sighed as they watched the car pull into the courtyard and right onto the grass. "Damn it, Ray, I just mowed that," Alistair grumbled.

"Close, close!" Rebecca urged the gate. An arm reached in and was severed as the gate shut tight. "They're safe, oh thank God, they're safe," she breathed, walking around for several seconds and then collapsing on the couch.

For the Moment

Krissy cried and laughed in the back seat. Ray's head was down on the steering wheel as he tried to get his breathing under control. Jen released the dashboard and flexed her fingers. She reached into her bag and tried to call her son again. Punching the end button, she gripped the phone, trying to strangle the small device as if it had done her personal harm.

"He knows where we are. He'll make it; I know he will," Ray whispered to his wife. He then turned to his daughter. "Shh, shh, sweetie, we're OK; we made it," he consoled her. Ray then turned to look at the house. He reached up to take the wheel and found he had no strength. Taking a deep breath, he tried again. His hand found the wheel. Ray pulled the car as close as he could to the front door, actually driving up three of the stairs onto the large front porch. He could hear his brother-in-law cursing him in his mind. The thought made him smile a little.

"Where is Kyle?" Krissy asked.

"He'll be here soon," Ray lied while helping her out of the car. Jen was already working on the code for the heavy steel front door. Large steel shutters covered all the windows on the ground level. They could hear sirens and chaos over the twelve-foot-high walls. Ray looked out at the gate. He noticed the severed limb and decided to steer his daughter to her mother's side. Several loud clicks issued from the front door, and with a great heave, Jen pulled it open. Ray noted it had to be a foot thick with heavy bolts that fit into large holes in the steel frame.

"Seriously paranoid," he muttered. "Good thing though, I guess." Jen didn't say anything but just tried her phone again. Krissy stood in the middle of the grand foyer, staring up at the balcony and staircase. Ray looked around and spotted the panel he was told to look for. Pressing the button, he heard it power up. It was black with only a small green light on the bottom. Slowly the picture showed the frowning face of his brother-in-law.

"Nicely done on the porch," Alistair grumbled.

"I knew you were going to say something." Ray shook his head.

Rebecca appeared in place of Alistair. "Jen, you guys make it OK? Anyone hurt?"

"Aunt Becca!" Krissy shouted.

"Hey, Kris, where is your mom?" Rebecca asked.

"Hi, Bec. Have you heard from Kyle?" Jen questioned.

"No. He's not with you?"

"No," Jen muttered miserably.

"OK, the place is locked down for now. Kyle will be able to get into the courtyard, but you'll have to let him in the front when he gets there," Rebecca told her sister.

"There are cameras set up all around the perimeter. The control panel and monitor selector is in the den," Alistair broke in. "There is plenty of food; if the grid goes down, you have at least two months' worth of fuel for the generator plus solar power. Water shouldn't be a problem with the well and purifier. You guys are safe. When Kyle gets there, we will know," he added.

"How will you know? Do you have cameras and mics all through this place?" Ray asked.

"Yeah, but I'm sure we'll hear Jen yelling at him," Rebecca tried to joke.

"This place is cool, Dad," Krissy said, walking in from another room. "You should see the huge TV."

Where To Next?

Kyle cursed under his breath. He could barely see out the shattered windshield, and now he was running out of gas. He pulled into a gas station and gave a whoop of excitement. There at the pump was a new yellow-and-black Chevy Camaro. The door hung open, and the inside chimed, telling him the keys were in it. Pulling up alongside it, he jumped out of his car and began to transfer his belongings.

He dropped his backpack, and a picture fell out. He threw the pack in the back of the car and picked up the picture. He looked down at his little sister's smiling face and remembered the little girl he threw the bottle at. Guilt filled him for a second. He tossed the picture into the car. Movement caught his attention. A man stumbled out of the convenience store. He wore a tie and sports coat. He held his neck, and blood covered half his face and the collar of the white dress shirt.

Kyle looked up at the man, who stretched his arm out. "What? Is this your car?" Kyle asked. "You don't want me to take the car?" Kyle asked, walking toward the man. "You need something from me?" He pointed the gun at the approaching man. The man only groaned and increased his pace toward the young man. "You want help? Or how 'bout I just shoot you in the face?"

The man groaned again, and Kyle shot him. "Fucking zombie," he spat. He kicked the body over and rummaged through the pockets. Pulling the man's wallet out, he opened it up. "Wow, dude, you were loaded." Pocketing the bills, he took out the credit card and returned to the pump.

He swiped the card and proceeded to fuel up the Camaro. "Looks like you already had that idea," Kyle stated as the pump clicked after only a second. "Let's get some more beer." Kyle took a step toward the store and then froze. "Nah, that is where you were. Looks like someone else is in there," Kyle addressed the body.

The tires skidded and caught as Kyle peeled away from the gas station and onto the road out of town. There was an iPod in a cradle, paused. Kyle unlocked it and hit play. "Kick-ass!" he cried as Metallica filled the speakers. Cranking up the music, he tore down the road. As the last note of "Call of Kathulu" still rang in his ears, another tune caught his attention as "Battery" began. Kyle slammed on the brakes and turned down the music. His phone was ringing. Fumbling in his jacket, he pulled it out and hit answer. His little sister's voice was in his ear.

"Kyle! Where are you? We're at Uncle Al's. We couldn't wait until you got home. Where are you?" she squealed into the phone.

"I went by the house, and it was all messed up. I thought they got you guys. You're at Uncle Al's?" he sputtered into the phone.

"I knew you were OK. Mom is all upset, and Dad keeps saying you're going to be here any moment. When are you going to get here? Are you almost here?" she pleaded.

"Like they care. They left without me," Kyle grumbled. "I'm fine, sis. I am on my way out of town." His anger at his parents returned to him, the anger he felt when he made it home through the anarchy to find the house empty and trashed.

"Kyle, I'm scared," she whimpered.

"Dad will take care of you." Kyle found he didn't want to talk to her. It hurt. He wanted to get out. He was free. No parents, no school, no rules. This was the end of the world. The zombies were walking the earth, and he was alive. He had a gun, a car, beer, food. What did he need a family for? Especially a family that never paid him any attention.

"Please, Kyle," she begged.

"I'll talk to you later, sis," he said and hung up. He stared down at the phone and hated what he had just done. "Best day ever," he muttered and kicked up gravel as he tore down the road again. He opened another beer. After several swigs, he tossed the bottle out of the window. Drinking had lost its fun for the moment. His sister's voice kept pleading with him. He noticed the twelve missed calls from his mother.

Twenty minutes later found Kyle staring at a crossroads. There were four choices in front of him. He could try to get to the highway to the right. He could stay straight and see how bad things were in the next town. He could go left to the state park. He could turn around and go back to his sister.

Darkness engulfed the car as the minutes ticked by. The headlights illuminated the signposts. He sat staring at the signs, his phone in his hand. It had been so easy to run away when he thought they were already dead. He flung the phone out the window.

It Looks Permanent

"Dad, Mom, I just talked to Kyle. He says he is leaving town." Krissy came running into the den. Ray looked from the TV to his daughter. Jen ran to her.

"Is he on the phone now?" she asked, grabbing the phone from her crying daughter's hand.

"Jennifer!" Ray exclaimed and hugged his daughter.

"What? She should have brought the phone to me so I could talk to him!" she shouted. "Damn it, Krissy, you knew Mommy wanted to talk to your brother!"

"That is *enough*!" Ray yelled at his wife as she descended on the little girl. Jen staggered and stared at Ray. "I pray to God he is OK. I wish he was here, but he isn't, and that was his choice! He left when we told him to stay, just like always. He always did what he wanted, and you never did anything about it! Every time he came home late, drunk, or whatever, you always let him get away with it. But you will not take this out on Krissy!" Ray shouted, glaring at his wife. "Speaking of her, when was the last time you even noticed what your daughter was doing?" In the stunned silence, he took his daughter by the hand, and they left Jen stunned in the middle of the den.

Ray had been annoyed about Kyle's discipline for a while. He wanted Kyle to get a haircut, didn't like his music, accused him of smoking, and didn't like his earring. Jen thought it was just a phase. He was a good boy, just experimenting. Krissy was fine. She always was. *What did he mean by not noticing Krissy?* she thought. It had been unfair to Kyle; he was seven and needed his mother, and she was pregnant. Krissy hadn't been planned, and Jen felt guilty that Kyle had gotten used to being the center of attention. Her thoughts were interrupted by a voice in the hall.

"Ray? Jen? Where are you guys?" Alistair called.

Ray walked over to the display and, running a frustrated hand through his hair, hit the "talk" button. "Yeah, Al, what is going on?"

"Everything OK there?" Alistair asked.

"Seriously? Do you have to ask? My son is missing, the dead are walking around, and we are locked in a house in the middle of a fucking burning city. No, everything is *not* OK!" Ray thumped his head against the wall.

Alistair stared into the monitor and grimaced. It had been a stupid question. "Sorry, I have been monitoring all the news channels." He sat, trying to figure out what to say next. Ray's face appeared on the monitor. Alistair took a deep breath. "The plague is everywhere. I have been listening to the military frequencies, and they are losing control. They are trying to evacuate the cities or just close them off. Your best bet is to stay where you are until they get things together."

Ray gave a small, humorless laugh. "I know things are bad when Alistair is telling me to wait for the army to figure things out."

"Listen, things look to be kinda permanent. So your best bet is to just sit tight. There is plenty of food and fuel. There is enough space around you, so if one of the houses next door catch fire, it will not spread to that house. Now just in case," Alistair hesitated, "there is a panic room in the basement. You can hold up there for at least a week." Alistair finished, wanting to say more but not knowing what to tell Ray.

Ray just stared at the man on the monitor. "Yeah, all right." He sighed. "I know you have hacked into the street cameras. Please keep an eye out for Kyle." Alistair nodded, and Ray walked away, head held low.

Not Just the Dead

Somewhere to the right, a window shattered. Mary Masse cowered under the desk, her fishnet stocking–covered knees pulled up to her chest. This was supposed to be a safe place; this was an evacuation site. The nice-looking young man who usually worked the front desk was lying on the floor in front of her. His eyes filled with terror as he clutched the gaping, freely bleeding wound on his neck. He reached out a hand to her. Mary gave a small scream and scrambled out from under the desk.

She made it three steps before a man rushed past her, knocking her into one of the benches. She threw out a lace-gloved hand to catch herself. Spinning, she watched as he made it to the front door. He started to push the door open when a woman in workout shorts grabbed him. He tried to push her away, but she was able to bite off three fingers from his hand. Screaming, he turned from the woman, only to have his bottom lip ripped off. A man in a business suit stood happily crewing on the lip. The man ran, screaming, into the arms of a group of them just outside the doors to the Y.

Bloody children streamed out of a doorway. Their small hands and teeth tore into the legs of several women who tried to help them. One woman lifted a child from the ground as it attached itself to her arm. It bit and growled like some rabid animal, clinging to the screaming woman.

Another man smashed a chair through the front window and attempted to flee. Mary watched as he ran to a car and fumbled in his pockets for the keys. Several of the creatures swarmed him. The car's alarm began to blare as the man slammed onto the hood. Mary saw his arm rise straight in the air, holding the keys; the alarm bleeped off.

A body fell from the balcony onto the tile of the lobby in front of her. Blood began to pool at her combat boot–covered feet. Mary felt her arm being grabbed. She screamed.

"Move, girl, we have to get out of here!" a woman screamed back at her while pulling her forward through the broken plate-glass window. The lady was fit, dressed in running gear. Mary did as little movement as possible, preferring to "contemplate life," so her savior was moving faster than she could. Mary stumbled through the doorframe and over the chair. The woman paused and then yanked her forward. Mary's shoulder felt as if it was being pulled from the socket, and her wrist screamed at the viselike grip. The cool air caused her to shiver. She was wearing a short black skirt and T-shirt; her leather jacket had been lost earlier. She kept brushing her long black-and-purple hair from her eyes.

"Slow down, I can't keep up," Mary whimpered. The woman didn't answer but pulled and dragged Mary as fast as she could from the front of the building. The glow of the bright lobby was lost to the gloomy lights of the parking lot. Cars were parked together in a chaotic mass. People had converged here in a hurry when it had been designated an evacuation zone. Mary tried to pull her hand free. "Thanks for your help; I have to go," Mary tried to explain.

The woman was scanning the area, looking for the best way out. Taking a step this way and that, not finding what she was looking for, she finally pulled Mary up onto the hood of a car and began to pick her way across the crumpled metal. Mary slipped over the smooth hood of a sports car. Wrenching her arm free, she was better able to steady herself. The woman glanced back but did not stop moving forward. Mary followed as close as she could. *She must be one of those crazy obstacle runners*, Mary thought. *Freaking obstacle Annie.*

"Annie" jumped, catlike, off the last car onto the grass between the parking lot and the road. She hissed and waved Mary forward. Suddenly all Mary could see was the road. She heard a soft thump as Annie jumped out of sight. "Come on!" a voice rasped from the darkness.

"I'm coming!" Mary hissed back.

A young boy clawed his way out from under a car. The skin above his right eyebrow was now hanging on his cheek, leaving thin blood trails as he staggered forward. He could see the silhouette between him and the well-lit road. Taking a few struggling steps forward, the boy groaned. Mary, dressed as she was in all black, disappeared into the ditch at the edge of the lot.

"Where are you, girl?" Annie's voice asked.

"Mary."

"I'd say nice to meet you, but under the circumstances..." A noise further down the ditch caused them both to freeze and stare into the darkness. A raccoon was briefly visible, running from the ditch in the pool of light from a streetlight. Across the street, a car door slammed and an engine revved. Tires squealed out of the lot as a woman came out of the building, screaming, "You have a duty to this station and to the state! Get back on that board!"

"Where are you?" Annie's hand grabbed Mary's, and she sighed in relief. "Come on! It must be safe over there." As if to urge them on, several screams and the sound of more breaking glass issued from behind them. Mary caught a glimpse of a young boy moving toward the ditch.

Annie's grip tightened. "Let's go!" Mary found herself being pulled out of the ditch, across the grass, and into the light of the road. She was surprised at how fast Annie could move as they sprinted across the concrete. Mary glanced back; she could see people milling about in front of the YMCA they had just left. She knew none of them were alive, and she hoped they didn't look over this way. Quickly as they could, Mary and Annie were off the road onto the grass in front of large windows spewing light.

"Not good, too much glass," Mary warned. Annie shushed her. They stopped at the corner, watching the screaming woman. She was standing several feet away in a parking lot, staring at the last place she had seen the taillights. She waited, clenching and unclenching her fists. "Get back here!" she yelled at the empty space. While she was yelling, another person ran past her. She made a mad grab for him.

"Get back in there!" she screamed.

"You're crazy, Diane! Go home to your family!"

"You have a duty to our viewers!"

"We're a public broadcaster, you crazy bitch! No one is watching us!" The statement was punctuated by a slamming car door. The woman named Diane was advancing on the car as it started.

"Get back inside or you're fired!"

"I quit! The dead are walking, and you're insane!"

Diane jumped out of the way of the screeching car. Stamping her feet and shaking her fists, Diane continued to scream, "After all we've done! You're fired! You'll all be fired! I'm going to the boss!"

Annie dropped Mary's hand. She quickly moved out of the shadows, hurrying toward the flailing woman. Annie held up her hands, trying desperately to calm her. Mary could hear the groans of the undead across the street. She was torn between running and staying with her companion.

"Shh, shh, they'll hear you!" Mary whispered while Annie was trying to calm the raging Diane. Suddenly feeling very alone and vulnerable without being dragged along, Mary started to panic. Looking quickly around her, she heard everything moving and coming at her. Something popped up out of the ditch and disappeared again. Mary was at Annie's side in an instant.

"Those ungrateful people…" Diane was growling but had calmed enough to notice where she was. Her eyes were darting around, searching the blackness outside the amber lights of the parking lot.

"Please, let's get inside. It's not safe out here," Annie coaxed. Mary was slowly edging her way to the door. She was sure there was something moving just out of the light of the lot. The shadows swayed and shook. Diane caught the look on Mary's face. She spun to see what had the girl so entranced.

"I see you! I see you. If you leave, don't bother coming back!" Diane screamed. Mary spun to face the road, catching the flash of a car as it sped away. More shadows seemed to be moving across the pavement.

"Seriously, it's not safe! We need to get indoors." Annie was trying to get Diane to focus. Fear was starting to overtake Mary. She strained her eyes until she was sure. Two of them were crossing the road. Mary waved frantically over Diane's head, pointing across the road. Annie's attention was completely on Diane, whose attention was on the back of the lot. Not wanting to make a noise but desperate to be seen, Mary jumped up and down, waving. Annie just waved her off, pulling on Diane's sleeve.

Throwing her hands up in frustration, Mary let her panic carry her to the glass front door. Grabbing the handle, she pulled with more force than she needed. The door swung easily, banging into the low concert wall that stood nearby. Mary didn't even pause as she ran into a small glass vestibule. Straight ahead was another door. Through it, there was a reception desk and a lobby. Mary grabbed the handle and heaved. Her fingers slipped, and she fell back, banging into the first door, causing a crack she had made when she opened it to grow longer. The door to the lobby—and hopefully safety—remained tightly closed, mocking her.

That crazy lady must have a way back in, Mary thought. She spun around, pressing her hands against the glass. Staring into the darkness of the lot, she could see Annie still motioning to the door as she took a few steps toward it. Diane was pointing at the road, arguing with her. Mary breathed out in relief as she saw that Annie finally had Diane moving toward the building.

Mary felt suddenly drained. She was so tired, her shoulders ached from tension. She sagged, rubbing her eyes. Turning back to the lobby, she noticed it looked deserted. That was good. The YMCA had been full of people and police and the army, and it was overrun in minutes. Fewer people had to mean fewer zombies. Anxiously she turned, willing Annie and Diane to hurry. Mary's warning was too late. She hadn't been watching their progress, and Annie was too intent on getting Diane to follow her; they never saw the lone zombie lunge from behind the ornamental bush.

"Bill! *No!*" Diane yelled. Blood sprayed across her face and the window. Mary jumped away from the gore-covered glass. She was transfixed with horror.

Annie's throat blossomed out a deep crimson that spread down her shirt. Her hands flew to the wound, trying desperately to stem the stream shooting between her fingers. Diane finally seemed to finally understand what was going on. Annie tried to push Bill away. Diane ran past him. She threw open the outer door and flung Mary aside. Annie was pressed against the glass, and Bill was tearing into her shoulder. Her eyes met Mary's. Annie began to slide down the window. Pulling the bloody hand from her throat, she pressed it to the glass. The look Annie gave Mary was filled with an apology, terror, and sadness. Bill lunged in again, desperate for another bite. He stopped, cocking his head to one side as if confused. Annie lay still. Bill's attention was now on the two women in the glass cage.

Diane fumbled for her keys, dropped them, cursed loudly, picked them up, dropped them again, stamped her foot, and grabbed them again. Mary's attention turned from the corpse that had been her companion to the one standing in front of her. Bill was bumping his hands and head into the glass. The loud cursing of Diane seemed to agitate him more by the second.

Diane was oblivious; she continued to curse and stamp her feet as she retrieved her keys for the third time.

"Shut up, he can hear you!" Mary warned. Bill's fist crashed against the glass, rattling the entire wall. Mary was now very aware of the broken glass in the door. She stumbled back in terror, slamming into Diane.

"Get off me!" Diane barked, pushing Mary off. Mary overbalanced and was thrown against the glass, face-to-face with Bill's dead, staring eyes. Mary grabbed the outer door and held it tight. The keys hit the floor again.

"Open the damn door already!" Mary cried.

"I'm trying, I'm trying!" Diane whined.

Bill's fist hit the glass again. Mary jumped back but held the door firmly. Behind her, she heard the key finally click in the lock. Bill moaned, slamming the glass again; the crack grew. Mary turned in time to catch the inner door before it shut. Diane was already halfway across the lobby. Mary was through the door, pulling it shut as fast as she could. Bill had stopped hitting the door, as it had splintered so much that he couldn't see Mary clearly. She backed away slowly, not wanting to recapture his attention. A slamming door caused her to spin on the spot. She was now facing an empty lobby.

"Bitch," she breathed. "*Bitch*!" Anger forced the word out in a yell. "You almost left me!" She immediately regretted it. Bill pounded on the glass door, shattering the rest of it. Terror turning to fascination, Mary watched as Bill was completely baffled by the metal bar running across the middle of the door that held the lever to open it. No matter how much he tried, Bill could not seem to figure out how to move forward. "Not very bright, are you? I guess you could be considered…brain-dead."

Mary laughed at her own bad joke. She jumped, pulling her attention away from the fumbling zombie. His phone was ringing and vibrating in her pocket. She had been trying it for hours when she was waiting to evacuate with no luck. Fishing it out of the tight skirt, she quickly crossed the lobby to a door at the far end.

"Hello?" she whispered while she peered cautiously through a small window that looked in at a hallway.

"Mary! Thank God! I've been trying to get through for forever! Where are you?"

Mary's brother Chris's voice burst from the speaker. Mary flinched and switched ears, pushing the door open as she whispered, "I'm in that TV-station thing across from the Y."

"Why are you there? Why aren't you at the Y? That is the rescue center!"

Mary glared at her phone. Her brother always had the amazing ability to annoy her. "Maybe because of all the zombies there! Where are you, then?" Silence followed her question. "Chris?" Mary pushed the door open and slipped through it. She quietly eased the door shut. Through the phone came a loud crash and a muffled cry. Mary strained to hear what was going on. "Chris?" she whispered. There was another crash and what sounded like a door slamming.

"Hold on," Chris hastily replied. A heavy thud, a start of an engine, and a quickly turned-off radio. "Stay where you are. I'm coming to get you."

Mary edged forward and stopped instantly, terrified. "Why? Why aren't you with Mom and Dad? Mom said you were going to the rescue center at the end of Londonderry. She was pissed because I was over here like I knew the dead were going to rise." Her mother was always pissed at her lately, Mary thought. "Kevin and I had this date planned." The last words caught in her throat. She had no idea where her boyfriend was or if he was OK. Then again, she had no idea why Chris wasn't with their parents either, if they were OK.

Shaking off the fear from her head, she turned a corner. An empty office stared at her on the other side of the hall. She passed another open door. This one looked into a room full of blinking lights, computer screens, TV monitors, and tape decks. Halfway down the hall was a window that looked into a room with a very large screen sitting in front of a board with buttons and lights all over it. On the huge monitor, some kind of manufacturing plant was being toured.

Mary watched the man explain how to make gas burners. Not wanting to know but needing to, she asked. "Why isn't Mom yelling at me?"

Chris sighed. "We never made it to the rescue center."

"Where are you?"

"I just left the neighborhood."

"Chris, where are Mom and Dad?"

"Dead." The silence that followed dragged on. Mary couldn't register what she had just heard. Somewhere down the hall, a door slammed. Mary's head snapped toward the sound. Chris spoke at last. "Listen, Mare"—a name she embraced yet hated—"just stay where you are. I'll be there as soon as I can. It is a mess out here."

"I'll be here," Mary whispered. The phone went silent. Mary hated the idea of being rescued by her brother. "The good twin," she spat out.

"I don't understand how twins could be so different," her mother would often say.

The angry frown faded from her face as the realization of what Chris just told her sank in. Her parents were dead. Her stomach clenched, and she grabbed the wall. Were they *dead* dead, or were they *wandering around* dead? she wondered and then immediately felt awful for thinking it. She prayed they were *dead* dead. She had not gotten along well with her parents for the last couple of years, but she had never wanted this. Looking from her black fingernails to the all-black outfit, she cringed. She did it to annoy them more than anything else.

Her guilt was cut short as a door at the end of the hall was flung open. Diane strode through, moving with purpose. Mary caught a glimpse of stairs before the door swung shut.

"I told him! I told him, the boss. I told him they all deserted us. I asked if I could fire them all, and he said yes!" Diane shouted while advancing on Mary. "I said they should be fired, and he agreed!" Diane laughed, grabbing Mary by the shoulders and shaking her painfully. "Fired…! Who are you? Get back on the switcher."

Mary broke free and began to back away. "Whoa, hey, I don't work here."

"That's right—you won't unless you get back on that switcher!"

"You…you told your boss everyone left? Is he still here?" Mary demanded as she continued to back away. Diane was still advancing on her. Mary stayed just out of reach.

"Yes, he's in his office upstairs. I said everyone should be fired, and he agreed! He always values my opinion. I can fire everyone, including you. Now, *get back to work*!" Diane's eye bulged as she screamed, lunging at Mary again.

That was enough. Mary pushed past the flailing woman and ran to the door to the stairs. She was through the door, taking the stairs two at a time. Spinning around on the landing, she saw Diane had not followed. Taking the last set of steps at a quick pace, she paused at the door at the top. There was a small window embedded in the door. Mary peered through it at an empty open area that held some cubicles along the walls; some chairs sat in the middle of the room like a conversation area, but farther down the room, she couldn't see.

Pushing the door open a crack, Mary heard the door at the bottom open. She backed away from the door and looked down at the floor below. Diane glared up at her. She threw her hands up. "Fine! I'll run the whole thing by myself, and why not? I always have, and I always will!" she screamed. Mary watched Diane storm out of sight. Returning to the door at the top, Mary pushed it open and stopped cold. The sight that met her eyes sent her heart to her throat.

To her left was a short hallway that led to a break room. She could see overturned tables and chairs in the darkened room. A dark red stain ran the length of the hall, and bloody handprints littered the wall. In front of her was the large common area. A huge dry-erase board on wheels was lying on its side, blood smears obscuring the smudged writing. Mary carefully picked her way through some overturned chairs, smashed computer monitors, and broken keyboards. In the middle of the room was the conversation area. The small couch was drenched in blood. Something that looked like an ear was on the floor just under it.

Standing next to the gore-covered couch, Mary whispered, "Hello?" She heard no response. *Didn't Diane just say she had talked to the boss?* Mary thought as she surveyed the trashed room. Cautiously she picked her way farther across the room. Kicking over a trash can, Mary cried out as she sprang back. Under the bin, still clutching a keyboard, lay a severed hand. Blood pooled behind the ownerless limb.

Thump.

The sound drew her attention. "Hello?"

Thump-thump. Silence…Thump…thump-thump-thump.

Mary eased to the corner of the blood-spattered end cubicle. Taking deep, calming breaths, she could taste the blood in the air. Blowing out the breath, she peeked around the corner. "Eek!" escaped her lips as she flung herself back around the corner, eye closed tight. Hands balled into fists, head back, she steeled her resolve. Slowly she peered back around the corner. It took a moment to realize what she was seeing.

A cable ran from the handle of an office door to a desk that was built into the wall and floor. The cable held the door shut tight. A narrow floor-to-ceiling window revealed the source of the thumping.

Standing at the window was what remained of a man dressed in a business suit that was now ragged and bloody. One gore-encrusted hand held the metal frame, and the other hung uselessly at the end of a mangled arm. His head wobbled back and forth on an exposed spine. The head barely held on by torn muscle and tendons. His head constantly nodded back and forth, bumping against the glass.

"Can I fire the staff?" Mary whispered. The zombie nodded, its head bouncing off the window. "Oh God, she's completely bat-shit crazy," Mary hissed. "Did the people downstairs know about this? Is that why they ran off?" Mary asked the dead man. She doubted it. The upstairs looked as if it had happened early in the day. She doubted the people who ran were even here when it happened. "And that bitch just let you come in…"

The crash of shattering glass spun her around. Mary collided with the door to the office. It moved. "Whoa!" she exclaimed, jumping away from the door. The bobblehead thudded harder against the window. Stepping forward, she grabbed the side of the cubicle. Her heart sank as she spied another hall that disappeared around a corner. "Oh God, oh God, oh God," Mary whispered under her breath, creeping to the next corner.

She was sliding along the wall, keeping her back to it, muttering as she went. "Why are you doing this? Run away, Mare, run away," she instructed herself even as she stood at the corner, preparing to look around it.

Wrapping both hands around the edge, she eased closer, inch by inch. She kept telling herself to run even as the hallway came into view. A long stretch of gray wall broken by a single picture of the mountains in fall met her gaze. She was looking straight down it now. Two bathroom doors stood off to the right; at the end was a brightly lit conference room. The door to the room was also held fast by a cable tied to the doorknob. She couldn't see where the other end was tied. The end of the hall seemed to split into a T. Two large floor-to-ceiling windows looking into the conference room. One side was completely obscured by vertical blinds. On the other window, the blinds lay in a crumple on the floor. Several of the high-back leather chairs were scattered around the room or overturned. A large, flat-panel TV lay smashed on the floor.

The overhead lights flickered. Instinctively Mary looked up at the fluorescent fixture. It hummed steadily back at her. A rustling in the blinds and a crash of something heavy somewhere down the hall returned her attention to the conference room.

"You know they are in there. Why are you hanging around, girl?" she chided herself again but couldn't make her legs move.

The lights flickered again, and the rustling blinds ripped from the wall and fell to the floor. Mary flung herself around the corner and flat against the wall. She knew by the pounding on the glass and the desperate moaning that they had seen her. She had only had a glance. *There must be six or seven in there.* They were bloody and torn—people in shirts and ties, business skirts, and suit coats.

The lights flickered again and then went out. Mary could hear the glass protesting in its frame from the relentless fists. Her heart slammed against her ribs in time with the pounding of bloody fists. She stood alone in the dark, listening to the moaning and pounding from the conference room and the dull thud from the boss.

Panic was building in her. She let loose a scream when the emergency lights flicked on. Across the room, she spied the door to the stairs. She sprang forward off the wall. In the dim light, she misjudged the position of the couch and fell hard; pain exploded through her. Her knees and palms burned from the friction with the commercial-grade carpet, and her shin stung from the thinly covered wood of the furniture.

Behind her, glass shattered. Scrambling to her feet, she flew to the door. It banged open; jumping several steps, she landed hard on the landing, her ankles and knees protesting at the abuse. Limping slightly, she thundered down the remaining stairs. Skidding to a halt, she rested her head against the door, desperately trying to catch her breath.

"Now I only have to deal with crazy," she panted. Breath froze in her throat as her heart stopped. The door above her creaked open. Mary pushed on the door in front of her. Panic swelled. Now her breathing was in short gasps, and her heart was pounding painfully again. Her door stood resolutely closed. She felt over the door; there was no bar to push. Looking down, she saw the handle.

"Why does this door have a handle?" she demanded. As she slammed down the handle, the door sprang open. Mary stumbled and slipped through. Spinning on her heels, she grasped at the metal bar. Something heavy crashed down the first set of stairs.

"Why the hell does this side have the bar? Who designed this place?" She pulled the door closed as best she could. In the stairwell she could hear the creature pulling itself off the floor, dragging itself toward the stairs. Moving away as quickly and quietly as she could didn't keep her from hearing something, or someone, else tumbling down the stairs.

"Break your bones. Crack open your skulls and die!" she growled at the closed portal. Closing her eyes, attempting to get her heart to slow down, she considered what she had learned. "They had trouble with stairs and doorknobs at the Y," she muttered. "Should be safe…ish for a while. As long as there are none down here…"

Mary knew she needed to get back to the lobby to wait for Chris. She now faced the long hall and a crazy woman who stood between her and her goal. Mary could see down the hall but couldn't tell where Diane was. A weak thud against the door urged her on. The dimly lit hall seemed to grow longer as she took each tentative step. The room with the large screen still had power; blue light spilled across the hall.

Mary realized she was holding her breath as she slowly and quietly crept through the large window into the room. She could see the technical equipment running, with some numbers ticking down while others ticked up. The screen now showed an interview show. The interviewer and the guest were discussing some obscure historical figure of the state's history. There was no one in the room.

"Does anyone actually watch this crap?" she muttered. Her luck held as no one was in the next room, either. A crack of plastic on plastic froze Mary at the doorway.

"Fine! Don't answer! You'll never freelance here again!" erupted from the office at the corner. Mary ducked into the room as Diane stormed out of her office and around the corner, away from the lobby, muttering, "Where is that damn intern?"

"She can't be talking about me," Mary gasped. "That bitch is seriously nuts." She waited a few seconds. Diane did not return. Seeing her opportunity Mary hurried toward the lobby. Checking around the corner, she couldn't see Diane. Mary eased the lobby door open, slipped through, and eased it shut. When she looked through the windows, the lot seemed empty. Bill was still on the patio, wandering aimlessly between the bench and the low wall.

Keeping low, Mary quickly slid under the long counter that made up the receptionist's desk. Scurrying into a corner where she couldn't be seen by the windows or from the hallway, she curled up into a ball. Clutching her bruised knees to her chest, Mary let several frightened tears fall. She had never wanted to see her brother more in all her life. She fumbled with the torn knee of her stocking and looked at her chipped black nail polish. She could hear the dead stumbling around above her. It felt like she had been here for hours. She wanted her mother. Mary still couldn't believe she would never see her again. The click of the hall door opening made her grab her knees and drew them closer to her.

"Where is the girl? I'm going to call her school and tell them that she is not to come back!"

Lights flashed through the lobby windows. Mary held her breath, willing Diane to go away. She was sure Chris had finally arrived. She prayed he had arrived.

"Who is that?" Diane demanded to the empty room, or maybe she was asking the dead or the voices in her head. Mary just wanted her to go away. Diane was crossing the lobby; the problem was she was not returning to the interior but heading to the outside door.

"Go away, go away, go away," Mary chanted quietly. Jerking, she banged her head on the underside of the desk when Type O Negative's "Black Number One" burst from her phone in her skirt pocket. "Oh shit!" Mary rolled out from under the counter. She crouched at the ready.

Diane spun on the spot to see where the music came from. Pointing an accusing finger, she screamed, "You were hiding! We have a duty to the viewers!" Mary stared at Diane, who stared back. Bill turned to face the glass, mouth open and teeth bared.

Time slowed. Mary's boot slipped her into a stumble on her first step. Her second was firm. She was around the counter and running for the door.

"Oh, no, you don't!" Diane screamed, moving to block Mary's exit. In an instant, Mary collided with both Diane and the door. The side of her head rang, and something warm and wet blossomed over her eye. White light exploded behind her eyelids, and her vision swam. She took a stumbling step toward the door. Diane was there, arms out. Mary lunged, and the two women spun, struggling for the door. Mary pushed Diane away, swiping at her eye; her hand came back red. Stunned, she gave Diane the opportunity she needed. Diane flung herself at Mary, catching her at the knees. Mary slammed against the door. The glass cracked, and pain shot through Mary's arms and chest. She bounced off the glass, but Diane was there with a second attack. Mary hit the door again, catching the release. They fell out into the cool night air and crashed onto the shattered glass.

Diane was stunned. Mary kicked free of her grasp and scrambled under the remains of the outer door. She slammed straight into zombie Bill, knocking him out of her way. Mary's head snapped back, her feet nearly leaving the ground. Diane had a handful of Mary's hair.

"You're not going anywhere, little girl!" she growled. Tears streamed down Mary's face as several hairs parted from her scalp. Chris was out of the car, screaming and running at them.

"I'll teach you the importance of hard wor*yyyeaaarrrrrccchhhhh*!" Blood sprayed across the patio. Diane let go of Mary's hair and grabbed at her own calf. Bill was chewing on a large chunk of Diane's leg. Grabbing Diane's arm, Bill began to pull himself up. They were face-to-face. Diane was furious. "Damn you, Bill! You've always been out—" What he had always been out to do was lost in a gurgled scream. Bill had stretched out, biting off Diane's lips and pulling half her cheek with them.

Mary fell back; arms grabbed her. She fought, screaming, against them. She was being pulled backward, away from the scene. Her feet kicked the air. Bill was on Diane's back. She was trying to claw her way back into the building. Bill's teeth sank into the back of her neck. Mary was screaming and kicking and punching, but she couldn't look away from the horror. She also had to get away from whatever had her.

"Mary! Mary! It's Chris. It's your brother!" he yelled. "Ow, damn it, that hurt. Come on, we gotta go!" Finally recognizing her sibling, Mary collapsed into his arms. Dragging her to the car, he threw open the door and pushed her in. Curling up and clutching her knees to her chest, Mary watched as Bill slowly rose to his feet, covered in blood. He stumbled toward the car.

The driver's door slammed. This was her dad's car, not Chris's. "Are you OK?" Chris asked as they squealed out of the lot. "Did you get bit? You're bleeding!" He reached in front of her, trying to steer and search the glove box. Pulling several napkins out, he held them against the cut over Mary's swollen eye. She slowly took over holding them.

After several minutes Mary was able to look over at him. He was dressed just as nice as ever. He looked as if he was ready for a day at school except for the bloodstains on his shirt and jacket. "Thank you," she whispered.

He glanced at her. "The highway is blocked; we'll have to go through town and try to pick it up on the other side."

"I want to go home," Mary whimpered. Chris swerved around several crashed cars. The silence was deafening in the car. "I want to…" Mary started a little louder, thinking her brother hadn't heard her.

"We can't," he stated. It seemed to take all his strength to finish "They're still there." Mary buried her face in her knees. Chris took the road back into town.

On the Road

Kyle sat in the car. The engine was running as he stared at the welcome sign. He was free. No overbearing Mom. No disappointed Father—but no sister, either. *She's a pain in the ass*, he thought with a smile that didn't stay in place. Thoughts of the old dirt bike he and his father had worked on when he was younger kept coming into his mind, along with images of his mom helping him with his homework.

"Dude, why are you even considering this?" he said out loud to the car. If he was truthful with himself, he already knew the answer. Because his life wasn't as bad as he pretended. He had been playing the misunderstood bad boy for so long that he was actually starting to believe he was as bad as he pretended. He laid his head down on the steering wheel again. "Dude, you're a middle-class kid from a decent family; get the fuck back to them."

His head snapped up as he was shaken from his thoughts by the sound of gunfire. He looked out the front window to the convenience store just ahead. There was an armored bank car in the lot, and a girl was shooting at an oncoming group of the dead. There were a couple of other people standing outside the truck now, firing at the crowd. He watched as they all ran back to the truck and drove away.

"At least I'm not stuffed in the back of that." He laughed as he surveyed the spacious interior of the Camaro. "And I look damn good in this." He sneered up at his reflection in the rearview mirror. "Ain't that right, baby?" he said, throwing the car in gear and running down the female zombie that was coming toward him.

He stopped to back up and run over her again, making sure she was completely dead. He grinned as he bounced over the corpse. He was still turned around when several hands slapped against the window. Kyle spun in his seat. Flipping his long hair out of his eyes, he sat in terror as the sports car became surrounded. It began to rock back and forth as they tried to get at him.

"Fuck! Fuck! Fuck this!" he screamed, flooring the accelerator. The engine whined, and the wheels spun as the car tore through the body beneath it. The high-powered engine pushed through the wall of zombies, finally gaining traction; bodies began to slide past. The wails of frustration rang in his ears from the damned souls that begged him to join them. Kyle screamed in jubilation at the car's freedom.

Tears streamed down his face, and his hands trembled on the wheel. He was heading back into his hometown. A sudden realization tore into his brain. He had no idea where his uncle's house was. He had a vague idea where it was, so he headed in that direction. *Damn stupid to throw out the phone, dummy*, he thought.

After driving around for a couple of hours, he was desperately trying to calm his growing panic. He had no food or water. All that he had were a couple of warm beers in the back seat. He drove up a long, winding road to the top of a hill that overlooked the town. It seemed deserted enough. He felt so tired. He rested his eyes for a moment.

Kyle groaned. His back was stiff and he had to pee. He mentally slapped himself for not pulling down the curtains in his bedroom, because the sun was burning in his eyes. He realized he was sitting up, and he was stiff and cold in the driver's seat of a sports car. "Shit, that actually happened," he mumbled, rubbing off the confusion from his eyes. The fog was slowly lifting around the car. The valley below was completely covered in a sea of white. A bird sang in a tree close by. It seemed so peaceful. How could the horrors of the last two days have actually happened?

Straightening up in the seat, Kyle realized he had a choice to make: use one of the empty bottles or get out of the car. He scanned the area, and it looked to be deserted. Slowly opening the door, he paused, listening hard, but his ears were met only by the sounds of morning.

Standing up next to the open door, he fumbled with his pants and began to take care of business. "Dude, how are you going to find this place?" he asked what was in his hands.

As he looked around, the fog began to evaporate around him. He was on the observation deck that looked out over the city. He remembered coming up here as a boy with his parents. Finishing up, he got himself squared away and hurried the short distance to the platform. His shoes made a hollow thump on the wood as he strode to the binoculars. Excitedly, he looked through the eyepieces.

"Shit!" he grumbled and searched his pockets for change. "Needs fifty cents." Finding only one quarter, he ran back to the car. Rummaging through the dash and seats, he found what he needed. Back on the observation platform, he looked out over the town. The fog was quickly burning off now, and the city began to be revealed. The ballpark was a blackened, smoldering shell. Several other buildings were still billowing smoke. "Holy shit," he gasped as he plunked the quarters into the viewer. He panned across the scene.

The park was full of the undead. Out to the east, the ramps to the highway were completely blocked. Shaking his head, he thought, *No, wait, the houses I need are not that way.* He panned back to the west. There! He focused on the historic district with its large brick houses.

"OK, so I'm looking for a big place with a wall," he told a squirrel that ran away. The thought of a huge old house made Kyle smile. He had always liked the big old gothic houses. "Probably haunted and shit. That would be cool." The smile slipped from his face. "Krissy wouldn't like that too much."

A noise from the trees across the road made his blood freeze. Kyle stared into the underbrush, straining his eyes. A rabbit scampered out of the bushes and across the road. Breathing a sigh of relief, he returned to his search. Finally, he located the section he was looking for. There were three—no, four potential places.

"OK, that is one seriously large bunny," Kyle said, not wanting to turn around. He patted his hips and realized he left the gun in the car. "That was stupid," he chastised himself, still not turning around.

Wishing desperately to see a deer, he began to slowly turn back to the car. A thump and then a dragging met his ears. "Deer don't limp," he said out loud. His gaze fell on a man. He might have been in his forties; he could have been twenty as far as Kyle could tell, as the man was a mess. Several holes in his shirt and pant legs told of being shot, but the tear across his cheek screamed of being bitten.

"Shit!" Kyle breathed as the man crossed the path back to the car. "OK, just run around the fucker—aw, nuts!" he spat as a woman slunk out of the bush. She raised her hands to him; a gun hung on one of her fingers, and the arm was bloodstained and bitten.

In a panic, Kyle ran away from the car, and the zombies followed. He turned to the woods but thought better of it, as his two new friends had just come from there. Changing course quickly, he ran past them toward the car. It was a smooth cut. *I should never have given up soccer*, he thought for a second. The driver's door still hung open, but he ran along the passenger side. Waiting at the back for a beat, he glanced back. It had worked; they were following toward the passenger side. He ran to the open door and jumped in, slamming the door shut and locking it quickly.

He hadn't run that far, but it felt as if he had run a minute mile. "Yeah, ya dumb fucks, ya can't get me now!" He turned the key, slipped the car into gear, and sped past the confused ghouls.

New Day, New Trouble

The sun was bright; the room held a chill, and Nikki's eyes hurt. The dark circles under her eyes contrasted the white of her knuckles on the phone. She had been awake all night. No one had come, no one had called, and no one answered. They had started moaning somewhere around midnight, one or two at first. The gunfire had died out not long after. The acrid smell of smoke still permeated everything. She knew someplace close by was still burning. She had seen them in the light it cast. They were in the tens by the four-o'-clock chime of the old church clock a block over. Now there was a stream of shambling, gore-covered undead.

The small radio she held to her ear to keep the volume low told her things were bad. There were evacuation sites she was supposed to go to. Through the night the list got shorter and shorter, with reports of lost communication. Before, there was just an automated recording, saying to stay tuned for further instructions; the announcer had said, "Survivors are urged to stay in their homes. Keep the doors locked and stay away from the windows. The National Guard will be going door to door to evacuate civilians. All first responders are to report to the following locations…" Nikki had given up on the radio not long after that.

The street in front of the store was now full of them—stumbling, shuffling dead. Nikki eased her fingers off the hard plastic, and the phone dropped into her lap. Her head drooped and then sprang up, eyes wide in terror. Had she just nodded off, or had she been asleep awhile? She checked her watch; it was barely seven thirty. She had just nodded off. Picking up the phone, she turned it over slowly, as if that would make it less disappointing. Still no calls; however, there was service. Fingers flew over the numbers—no answer; the next set of digits—no answer. After several failed attempts, the phone voiced its need for power through a series of angry beeps.

Crawling through the store, Nikki found her goal: a display of phone chargers. As she pulled one down, her shirt got snagged on a peg. Several items clattered to the floor. Nikki froze. Several hands, faces, and bodies collided with the front window. Rolling onto her back, she watched the ceiling and prayed for them to go away.

Watching

Alistair sat in the middle of his couch, watching the world fall into chaos. His multiple satellite receivers with several hundred channels from around the globe had steadily been going dark throughout the day. China was the first to go to black. He wasn't sure if it was due to the undead or the state-controlled media. He had been amazed at how different the Chinese news had been from the rest of the world. They had contended the entire time that there was no illness in the countryside and for the population to leave the cities in an orderly fashion until the government could sterilize the areas.

Alistair had wondered what "sterilized" had meant until a report from Korea made it clear what the Chinese had planned. Several large metropolises had been wiped from the map. China had used some of its nuclear arsenals on itself.

"Nice to see you're comfortable," Rebecca commented as she came around the couch.

Alistair looked up at his wife and sighed. "China nuked itself. Can you believe that?"

Rebecca slumped down next to her husband and picked up the remote. "I thought it would be North Korea," she noted, changing over to the BBC.

"No, they have said nothing. They are still doing the normal stuff as if nothing were happening there," he replied, scratching the stubble on his chin. Rebecca watched the BBC for a few moments. London was in flames, and the military was trying to get the living out.

Alistair rubbed his eyes and looked at the screen. "What station is this?" he asked, as there was no announcer describing the scene. Then it hit him. "Good Lord, is that downtown?" he gasped.

Rebecca had switched over from the BBC and was now going between several traffic cameras and then to a few security cameras they had hacked into. "What the hell are they doing?" she muttered, watching a group of people on the top level of the parking garage next to the hospital. "Oh, they need to get moving!" she said as she moved to the edge of the couch.

"They were there all night," Alistair noted, but he, too, had moved to the edge. "Hey, get out of there!" he called, knowing full well that the people in the armored car couldn't hear him.

"Oh shit, here they come!" Rebecca pointed at the screen. Zombies began to stumble up the ramp onto the top of the parking structure.

"Go, go, *go!*" the couple screamed in the softly lit living room with the seventy-two-inch LCD screen and comfortable microfiber couch. They held hands and gasped as the truck started to move. The zombies had now surrounded it. Several were flung off as the vehicle swung wildly around and dropped out of sight down the ramp. With a huge sigh of relief, the husband and wife slumped back on the couch and then turned to look at each other.

"I really think I hate this new reality TV," Alistair said with a sigh. "See if you can find Kyle. I'll go make some coffee," he added, getting up. He gave his wife a kiss and wandered back to the kitchen. The guilt of being so protected while watching others fight for their lives sat heavy in his stomach.

Shaking his head, he stood up straighter as he entered the gleaming gourmet kitchen. "I knew something like this was coming. Most people just buried their heads in the sand and trusted the government. It's not my fault—I just planned better." Scanning the packed pantry, he located the coffee shelf and selected an open container. He only felt slightly better.

Finding a Friend

The fog had completely lifted now, revealing what should have been a clear, sunny day. Instead, the sunlight was dimmed by the smoke from the still-burning fires. Kyle was painfully aware of how hungry he was. He needed to find something to eat—and his parents. His uncle was one of those survivalist nuts, as Kyle's father put it. For years he had been prepared for a military assault or a government breakdown, so zombies shouldn't be a problem for whatever defenses Alistair had put in place. Kyle tried to remember what his uncle had done to make money. All he knew was that Uncle Alistair had a lot of it—and spent a lot of it on his bunkers.

"I bet Dad no longer calls him a nutbag." Kyle laughed. A frown creased his face. "Now all I have to do is find the place." He tried to remember if they ever visited the house as he drove through the empty streets of a neighborhood. It had to be one of those big old houses he had seen. *It had to be walled off; it just had to be. So all I need to do is find the tallest wall with barbed wire and spikes*, he thought as he passed a house whose manicured lawn was rutted by the tires of a car that now sat in the living room.

His stomach gave a loud grumble as he stopped at the end of the block. He sat waiting, staring up at the stop sign. "Dude, it's a stop sign, so it's not going to turn green, and what the fuck? Not like a cop is going to give you a ticket." He laughed at himself. "Man, I need something to eat."

Slowly he pulled into the driveway of the nearest house. The front door was open. "Well, that will make it easier." He shrugged. Looking around, he noticed it seemed deserted enough. The streets were empty. He wasn't sure if this made him more uncomfortable. *Where did everyone go?* he thought.

He killed the engine and eased the door open. Cautiously he crept toward the door. Smiling, he clicked off the safety; he had remembered the gun this time. Pushing the door clear with a shaking hand, he entered the front hall. A kitchen stood off to the right that opened up into a living room. A short hall led to the left and what looked like bedrooms. All the doors were closed down the hall.

Ignoring the closed doors, Kyle went straight to the kitchen. Opening the refrigerator, he refrained from shouting as he grabbed an apple and some bread. He devoured the apple and rummaged through the fridge drawers, where he found some lunch meat. As he made a sandwich, a cat leaped onto the counter. Kyle yelped; grabbing his gun, he pointed it at the mass of fur. It rubbed against his hand. Rolling his head on his shoulders, he shook off the tension and then returned to making his meal. He sat for a moment, petting the cat and eating his lunch. He pulled a little piece of meat out and offered it to the cat. He smiled as it ate happily from his hand. Grabbing another apple, Kyle decided to check out the rest of the house.

The cat followed him as he walked down the hall and tried the first door. "Hey, little dude, watch our backs," he whispered to the cat as he turned the knob. It opened into a bedroom, a young boy's by the look of it. Several cartoon posters hung on the walls, and action figures were scattered over the floor.

He tried the next door. It was locked. He pressed his ear to the door and heard nothing. He gave the door a soft knock and listened. Still silent on the other side. Pulling a small knife from his pocket, he worked it between the door and the frame until it clicked and the door opened slightly. Looking in he saw the bathroom. The window next to the toilet was open, and bloodstains ran down the wall. Not looking in the tub, he closed the door and made sure it was still locked. The cat was at the end of the hall, staring at him.

It mewed softly as he approached the door. Kyle finished the apple and threw the core aside. He wiped his hands on his pants and retrieved the gun from his belt. He slowly turned the knob and opened the door. The sight that met his eyes stunned him. On the blood-soaked bed was a man. He was naked and tied to the headboard and footboard. He struggled to free himself as Kyle entered the room. The man made no sound, as his lower jaw was missing. The cat at Kyle's ankle hissed at the sight. Kyle only laughed.

"Well, either you were turning and your family tied you up to be safe, or you died doing some really kinky shit." Kyle froze as the sound of a chair falling over from the kitchen made the cat jump. The man on the bed was more agitated, thrashing wildly against his restraints. Kyle raised the gun and turned to go back down the hall. Two zombies entered the hall; the cat hissed at Kyle's ankle.

"Not to worry, little dude; watch this." Kyle smiled down at the cat and raised the gun. He fired, and the zombie on the left fell backward and did not move. Kyle sighted in the second zombie, pulled the trigger, and…nothing. He pulled back the chamber to clear the misfire and saw he was empty.

The cat was backing away, as was Kyle. The zombie was approaching quickly. Stiff legs carried it ever closer. Kyle's hands dipped in and patted at his pockets, only to find a few loose bullets. He stumbled into the bedroom. The tied zombie was now making a gurgling sound and had freed one hand by tearing it apart to get it out from the restraint. Its thumb lay on the bed, and two fingers dangled loosely on sinew as it grabbed at the air.

Kyle looked back at the door as the zombie approached. His foot slipped out from under him; a small, furry flash crossed the floor. Kyle was painfully on his ass. "Dude!" he yelled at the retreating cat he had just fallen over. He was lying against the bed. The zombie approached from the hall. Above him, a creature struggled to free itself further. He could hear the anger and frustration in its gurgling moans.

Feverishly Kyle again patted down his pockets. Panicked fingers grasped in his pockets. Three bullets scattered across the floor; he still held two in his palm. Pulling back the chamber, he tried to get the bullet in. The zombie loomed over him as he got the shell loaded. Shaking he aimed at the zombie. It was barely a foot away, leaning toward him, mouth open, a black hole guarded by gray teeth. He could smell the death emanating from it. He fired; the zombie stumbled back and fell against the dresser. *Jesus, that thing got rotten in a hurry*, Kyle thought as he wiped the sweat from his face.

As his panic calmed, Kyle became aware that something was on his lap. Picking the object up, he examined its pink, spongy texture. Turning it over, he saw the nail; it was one of the fingers from the zombie above him. Looking up he saw the other finger about to drop off the mutilated hand.

He was instantly on his feet, staggering away from the bed. Realizing he still held onto the finger, he cried, "Dude! Sick!" Flicking the finger across the room, he yelled, "Shit!"

The zombie on the floor began to crawl toward him. Quickly Kyle loaded another bullet and fired. This time the bullet found its mark, and the ghoul's head slumped forward, blood and brain oozing on the rug. A tearing sound from the right caused Kyle to look back over his shoulder.

The bone of the tied zombie's leg was starting to show. The flesh was separating from its other wrist as it fought to get free. Its hand slapped at the bed, sending the other finger flying at Kyle's head. The cat hissed from the corner. Kyle batted down the digit and then grabbed for a loose shell off the floor. He grabbed the first finger again, yelped, threw it again, and pick up a bullet. He loaded it but stayed his hand. The knee of the zombie was beginning to separate from the lower leg.

Bent over, quickly gathering the last two bullets, Kyle straightened up. He backed out of the room, quickly calling for the cat. "Dude, Dude Cat, come on, we're leaving!" The cat followed him out of the room. Kyle pulled the door closed. The cat watched his movements. Together they hurried down the hall. The cat paused at the front door as Kyle ran through it. Out in the street, he saw it was no longer deserted. The cat meowed plaintively from the door but would not follow.

"Dude! *Dude*! Come *on*!" Kyle yelled and patted his leg, urging the cat to follow. Several zombies were converging on the house now. "Shit!" he cried. He stepped toward the car, hesitated, ran forward, and scooped the trembling cat out of the doorway. The bed zombie had extracted itself from the room, leaving most of its limbs behind. Kyle watched, reminded of the Terminator at the end of the first movie. A nip on the chin from the cat told him he was wasting time. Running for the car with the cat over his shoulder, he dodged a couple of the undead. Wrenching the door open, he tossed the little creature onto the passenger seat and slammed his door shut. As he turned the key, the engine roared into life. He backed over a zombie and tore through the lawn.

The cat was standing on its back legs, looking out the window. "Dude, what the hell? You need to learn to come when I call you," Kyle admonished the cat. It turned to look at him and gave a small "Merrow" as it sat back on the seat. It seemed to be hanging its head. Kyle looked at the cat. It looked back at him with sad eyes. "Apology accepted," he sighed, "but don't hesitate again you big fraidy cat." He scratched it behind the ears, and the cat purred loudly.

Do Something

"I don't know! Hack into the road-construction signs! Make all the lights point to the house! Do something to get him here!" Jen screamed at the monitor.

"Jen, you're not helping," Rebecca stated calmly. "Alistair has tried to do all those things and more. The problem is, the power is out in some areas, and the lines are down in others. We can't access the road-warning signs, and even if we did…it might not be Kyle who shows up."

"Have you seen other survivors?" Ray asked. "Why wouldn't we want to help them?"

"Well…" Alistair began tentatively, "some of the things we've seen haven't exactly put some of the survivors too far above the zombies." Alistair paused, not sure if he should explain. "I watched a camera from the park. This guy killed two other people for their camping stuff." He sighed and continued, "I think you'd be better off with just people you know."

"No! That is crazy. We have food, water, shelter, and safety. How can we not try to get as many people here as possible?" Ray demanded.

"I don't want as many as possible; I just want my son!" Jen shouted from behind him.

"I want him here, too. But we can't ignore other survivors. People need to help each other now more than ever," Ray started.

"Ray, that is not the best idea…" Alistair interjected.

"And if we open this place up, maybe someone will know where Kyle is hiding, or where others are, and Kyle could be with them. Or—" Ray was cut off by an angry shout from Alistair that was quickly cut off by Rebecca.

"Or maybe they could kill you and your family! Ray, listen, you're going to attract enough attention soon enough when the power goes out in the rest of the city, and you still have lights on. You need to think about what to do if others want to get in by force," Rebecca explained.

"You're both just paranoid, you know that, right? Crazy paranoid." Ray shook his head.

"Well, you're safe because we are! And we were right!" Anger overtook him. Alistair flipped off the camera and sat glaring at the blank screen. "Ungrateful assholes," he spat.

"Yes, but they are worried about their son," Rebecca soothed.

"They do know he is dead by now, right?" Alistair stated, not wanting to believe it himself. Rebecca just rubbed her husband's shoulders, not wanting to confirm his statement.

Finding a Way

"You know I used to actually like mowing the lawn. It was cool. You saw that you actually accomplished something, and no one bothered you while you did it. You could pretend you couldn't hear them yelling over the mower," Kyle informed Dude Cat. He chose the name as he called him Dude anyway. The cat stared attentively at him. "I like that you listen. Good attribute to have."

They turned down yet another blocked road. Kyle had been trying for an hour to get to the house he believed was the one his family was in. Having to turn around again, he was getting more frustrated and even more lost. "OK, so if we turn around, then we turn here…" He edged the car around a corner. He smiled triumphantly at the cat. "We should end up next to the pa—" Kyle slammed on the brakes. "How the fuck did we end up at the river?" he yelled. The cat gave an angry yelp and jumped into the back seat. "This isn't my fault!" Kyle screamed at the small animal. It meowed mournfully back.

Tears streamed down Kyle's face as he pounded the steering wheel. "This isn't my fault! They left me, they left me," he wailed. The cat nudged his arm. He looked into Dude's eyes and began to pet him. "No, you're right. You're right…" He sniffed. "If I wasn't pissed at Dad, I never would have snuck out."

"Meerow?"

Kyle sighed. "And I would have been home when I was supposed to."

"Yerrowl," Dude Cat responded.

"Yeah, OK! It was stupid. I was being a punk. So what can I do now except try to find them?" he asked.

"Yerrowl! Mmmerrrowl!" Dude was staring out the front window. Several zombies had appeared in the street.

"Right. I see them." Kyle backed the car up and turned down another road, heading back into town.

Comes Out in the Wash

"I'm sorry," Ray said to his wife as he walked into the room.

Jen did not turn to look at her husband. She just kept changing the cameras. "I smothered him and ignored you and Krissy. It's my fault he ran off." She sniffed.

"I never let him do anything. I was too hard on him and made him think I loved Krissy more than him," Ray said to his shoes.

Jen was in his arms. "He'll find his way here, and we will make it right." She sobbed. Ray nodded and kissed her head.

Krissy entered the room and promptly exclaimed, "Ewww!" The couple turned and pulled their daughter in close. She was confused by their tears. "Is Kyle OK?" she ventured.

In the Bunker

"OK, that is the third time that car has passed that camera," Rebecca noted. "They have got to be trying to find a way to the house, I'm sure of it. Do you think that is…"

Alistair was busy at the computer. "I got a freeze, and I am trying to clear up the picture." The keys tapped under his fingers. "That's got to be him!" Alistair shouted. "Long hair and the nose looks like your sister's!" He pumped his fist at his side. "That's it, boy; now, let's get you to the house."

Rebecca was next to her husband on a second keyboard. Together their fingers flew over keys. "I hope the lights are still working in that area," she said.

"I'm on the cameras—yep, looks like we still have power!" The couple smiled at each other and returned to their typing.

In the Car

Kyle drove past the third flashing red light. He looked over at the cat and slowed. "OK, is that weird?" he asked. Dude looked out the window and meowed. The light flashed red. He looked to the right; it was red and flashing, but to the left, it was flashing green. He pulled forward slightly. The light flashed yellow and then red. He turned to the left, and the light went solid green.

"No fucking way!"

"Merow!"

Kyle followed the solid green lights. Left, right, left, straight. Dead stop.

In the House

"Mom, Dad, if you are done being gross, who's that?" Krissy pointed to the camera that looked down at the side street. There sat a car that hadn't been there a half hour ago. Switching to the camera at the front, Jen let out a small scream. There were several zombies blocking the path to the gate.

"It's him! It's him!" Jen was hopping up and down.

"Krissy, stay in the house! Jen, come with me!" Ray shouted and headed into the hall. Throwing open the closet, he pulled out a shotgun.

"What are you going to do? You've never shot a gun in your life!" Jen shouted to her husband.

"I don't know, but we have to give him a chance!" he yelled, heading out the front door. "I'm going up on the wall. I'll tell you when to open the gate." He was on the ladder as she ran out to the front gate. Neither saw Alistair waving frantically from the monitor.

End of the Line

Kyle pulled the car around the front and saw the way was blocked by several of the undead. "What do we do now, Dude Cat?" As if to answer his question, a zombie blew apart. Parts pelted the front of the car.

"OK! This *must* be the place then!" he yelled. Dude Cat was on his hind legs again, staring out the front. Kyle whispered, "I hope they are shooting at the zombies." Dude purred reassuringly.

The ground next to a zombie shot gravel into the air. Kyle looked up at the wall, trying to see the shooter. He spied the barrel of the gun and who was holding it. Kyle sat in total shock, Dude nudging his elbow. To Kyle's utter astonishment, his father was aiming. He watched the gun buck and his father stumble out of view as a second zombie blew apart. Kyle watched as his father appeared to regain his footing, waving Kyle on to the gate. He hit the gas, knocking a couple of the dead out of his way.

"What the hell does Uncle Alistair have loaded in there, huh?" Kyle steered toward the gate, running a third zombie down. The gate began to open as he approached. Several blasts from the gun blew off the arm of a zombie and knocked another off its feet.

Kyle had just enough space; he forced the car through the opening. The metal screamed as it scraped through. Dude hid in the back seat again. For the second time in as many minutes, Kyle was stunned by what he saw. As he squeezed through the gate, he saw his mother at a panel, punching buttons, and his father sliding down a ladder.

He was through, but so was a zombie. Kyle jumped out of the car, torn as to whom to run to first. His father ran forward, screaming. Kyle watched his mother run from the zombie that had followed him in.

Ray fired and missed the oncoming ghoul. His mother tripped; his father cried out. Kyle grabbed the shotgun from his father and ran at the zombie. The heavy wooden butt crashed down on the head of the undead. It twitched but lay lifeless at his mother's feet.

A few moments passed with only the moans of the ghouls outside the gate. Kyle stared down at the zombie and then held out his hand to help his mother up. She grabbed him and held him tight. Ray slammed into his son, hugging both Jen and Kyle tightly. Kyle gripped them both tightly as a third thump hit him lower, and he saw his sister's tearstained face staring up at him.

Alistair watched the monitor as the family reunion occurred. Wiping a tear from his eye, he looked over at his wife. "You big softy." She smiled and hugged him.

"They are all safe…for now." He sighed.

Closing Sale

Nikki was sick of snack food. She was tired of washing in a sink. She had had enough of lukewarm drinks, and she couldn't stand staying in the store any longer. The problem was, the crowd outside was not the welcoming kind. Well, they were, actually, but the kind of welcome that would kill you. After the second day, the power went out; by the third day, even the emergency light was gone. It had been a week, maybe more now. She had read through most of the magazines, was avoiding the romance novels, and had worn out the dial on the portable radio she found. By this time even the automated voices had gone silent.

She remembered reading *The Diary of Anne Frank* when she was younger. At the time Nikki couldn't imagine having to be silent for hours on end. Now she understood that other young woman's plight. During the day, Nikki stayed in the cramped, dark, windowless office. If she was spotted, the creatures would pound and bang on the windows and doors. Their howls would draw more and more to the shop. Cracks had already appeared in several panes of glass. One frame showed signs of coming loose. The first time she was spotted, they would have gotten in if not for an unfortunate group of people who turned down the wrong street. She didn't see what had happened to them. Their screams chased her back to the office, where she stayed for two days.

At night things were a little better. She could move around a little more, collect a few distractions for the next day. During this night she spent most of her time staying out of sight and quiet. She tried not to notice the dwindling supply of liquids in the row of dark refrigerators. The water had stopped running several days ago, so she started using the bottled water to flush. After a day she noticed how fast the bottles were disappearing. Lately, she'd been using diet colas. She had tried the milk products, but after a few hours, they became rather nasty.

With nothing to do but read about celebrities who probably weren't alive anymore, sleep, talk to a couple of stuffed animals, and think, Nikki started to form a plan. "OK, Mr. Bear, we need to get out of here."

"Yes, but where will we go?" she spoke in a gruff low voice.

Taking in a squeaky voice, she looked at a large stuffed mouse. "Hey, Nikki, didn't you comment once that there were windows above the store?"

"Yes, I did," Nikki replied to the plush animals. Dispensing with pretense, she stood up. "There must be a way up there." The animals just stared back with their blank, plastic eyes, but their sewn-on smiles encouraged her. "You're right. We need to find out what is up there. Maybe a real bed or a safer place to hide." She was looking at the door to the storeroom. "Or a way out of here. God, let it be a way out."

The storeroom was dark. Any windows that might be there were covered by boxes. Nikki found a ladder but had no idea where to start looking. She moved several boxes at the back, thinking she knew where the exterior walls were on either side. All she discovered was a steel door that appeared to be welded shut. There was a peephole in it, so she took a look. "That's great," she muttered. "It's the back door, and there doesn't seem to be anyone around." She gave the door a swift kick. "I don't have a blowtorch to get through it!"

She jumped, stumbling over a box of empty bottles as something heavy hit the door. Nikki looked back out through the tiny portal. Immediately jumping back again, she swore. Gray-green teeth showing through stretched, bloody lips chomped at the tiny hole. "Good job!" She slapped herself on the forehead. "Brought 'em right to you, dammit."

The sound of shattering glass ended all self-admonishment. Her heart was frozen in her chest. "Please be looters. I can deal with looters. I want it to be looters," she breathed as a tear ran down her cheek. She willed her feet to move. Her hands shook, her chest ached, and panic threatened to take over. "It's looters; I know it's just looters," she whimpered, her cheeks damp with tears and her forehead with cold sweat. The door creaked slightly. Peering through, she covered her mouth to keep from screaming. More glass fell as body after body fell through. Displays were knocked aside; merchandise spilled across the floor. Silently she closed the door. As she took two steps back, her foot hit a bottle; her balance was compromised as the bottle clattered across the floor. Not waiting, Nikki scampered up the ladder.

She crawled under the drop ceiling. The wires holding the grid up protested. Her flashlight caught a gleaming metal ring. Judging the distance, she knew it was out over the store. Slowly she crept to the top of a wall dividing the storefront from the back room. She could see down into the office. Her two stuffed friends had already been knocked aside by the shambling dead. More of the creatures poured into the room by the second. She wondered if they could smell her. She could smell herself, and it was only getting worse with the fear and perspiration. She wished she had turned off the small lantern so she couldn't see the horde below her.

Hating the undead and crying every second, she inched closer to the ring that she prayed led to a door to the upper level. A wire gave way, as did a cry from her. A ceiling panel crashed to the floor, and moans filled the hole. Blood seeped from cuts on Nikki's hands. She gripped the metal with all her strength. Her muscles ached, her eyes were shut tight, and her nose was filled with the dust on the tile that her face was now pressed to as she tried to block out the groaning from her ears.

The entire grid shook, and another support gave way. Nikki added a scream to the cacophony of sounds from the undead. Metal bit at her clothes and scratched at her skin. Tiles fell on the outstretched hands. More displays tumbled over under the crush as more and more of the undead spilled into the store. Her finger snaked into the ring and heaved. A door opened out of the ceiling. She was on the backside. A set of stairs unfolded out, smashing into the support grid. A small handrail was all that saved Nikki from crashing down with it.

As she hung on with her blood-slicked hands, hands now clawed at her shoes. The ladder had smashed several of the zombies that did not allow it to open completely. Kicking away the grasping claws, she got a foot on the steps. She was up and through. Even though she pulled with all that was left of her strength, the door barely moved. Zombies stumbled and climbed on each other, adding their weight to the problem. Body after body crashed into the old wood of the stairs.

Screaming with exertion, Nikki pulled; wood splintered, and zombies tumbled over each other. The door slammed shut, throwing Nikki flat on her back, the breath knocked out of her. Lying there gasping, she could see she was in a low room. The windows she had seen from the outside were spilling pale light into the empty space. The tears came fast and didn't stop for a long time.

Welcome Home

The car was running very low on gas. Chris and Mary had taken turns sleeping after the first day of driving around. Chris snored softly in the back seat. Mary stared out the front window at the empty street. They had backed up into a concrete enclosure that was used to hold dumpsters. It still stank of garbage, but it afforded safety on three sides—they hoped.

Mary had finally convinced Chris to go back to their house. She had to see for herself. When they arrived, the neighborhood was unrecognizable. Luggage, boxes, and furniture littered the street. Crashed and abandoned cars were across the road, on lawns, and several were embedded in houses. Signs of violence were everywhere. Red stains were on the sidewalks and sides of houses and doors. To Mary's relief—or horror—they found their house had burned at some point. The neighbor's house seemed to have blown apart, setting theirs ablaze. The two burned corpses on the front lawn could have been anyone, but Chris seemed to be content that it was their parents.

Every Christmas, Thanksgiving, and birthday came back to make her smile, immediately stolen by every fight, every moment of resentment and time she felt put upon. So many of those times felt so useless, so needless and stupid; who cared now if she didn't get to stay out as late as some of her friends did? She was an orphan and homeless. She never could go home, never argue with her parents about music or how she was dressed or about her friends. Unconsciously she took off the skull earrings and dropped them out the window. She had seen enough death without wearing them.

"You OK?" Chris asked sleepily from behind her.

Mary realized she was crying. "Yeah, I just…you know."

"Yeah, I do." He gave her shoulder a squeeze that turned from comfort to warning. She saw them. Three of the undead had shuffled in front of the car. They stood there, swaying back and forth but not advancing. "Get ready to get out of here," Chris whispered.

Mary's fingers found the ignition. The moment they decided to investigate was the moment they were going to taste the hood. Neither side breathed—one not daring to, the other not needing to. The howl caught Mary by surprise, but by the third one joining in, they were inches from the bumper. The sound was gone in the crunch of bodies on and under the car. Mary swerved, attempting to rid the front of the vehicle off the half zombie now trying to pull itself toward the window. Metal screamed as the fender met the guardrail. The body rolled off the hood into the darkness.

"Shit, I fucked something up!" Mary yelled. She was having a hard time steering.

"Head down Market Street, and we can try to find another car there." Chris pointed over her shoulder. Mary fought the car for a block. By the second block, the grinding was calling to every undead in a mile radius. The car barely staggered. "Screw it!" Chris yelled over the dying machine. "We gotta run!" A crowd was growing behind the car.

"No, there are too many," Mary protested, seeing their path beginning to be blocked.

"It is no good. The car is fucked." Mary knew things were bad. Chris rarely swore. "Down there!" He was pointing to an alley. Mary protested. "Mare, come on. See the fire escape? We can get to it from that dumpster." Chris barely paused, throwing open the door.

Mary still protested even after her door was wrenched open and she was dragged out. "We need to stay with the car. It is safe in there." She was pushed onto the dumpster. "This is a bad idea." The zombies were at both ends of the alley. "Chris! Let's get back to the—OK, OK, stop pushing." The ladder was within reach, and Chris was forcing her onto it. She was on the first landing as Chris pushed the dumpster away as best as he could. It bumped into a zombie that stood, confused, looking at it.

Mary screamed. The torn face of a woman was staring out of the window. Chris was behind Mary, pushing her further up the stairs. "This is no good! We gotta find something else!"

Chris ignored her. The next landing seemed clear. He tried the window; it didn't budge. The din from the undead was getting louder. Many were reaching for the bottom of the ladder that was, thankfully, out of their reach.

The glass was shattered where Chris kicked in a window. The sash was thrown up, and Mary was pulled through. Two doors stood on either side of the hall. Mary pulled Chris back as one opened a crack. An eye peeked out, followed by a beckoning hand. The twins rushed into the apartment. The door closed and locked behind them. Several people sat in the living room, staring at them as they stared back.

"Welcome to my home," a woman greeted them. "I think we are safe here."

Escape

By the second day, the smell in the attic was almost unbearable. Nikki was hungry even with the stench. This was second to her thirst. She could see the water below her, watched as the bottles were kicked over by the crowd of zombies still milling around. Few had been able to figure out how to get out after they forgot she was there. Her world consisted of three large windows on the front of the room and one smaller one on the side. She had looked out those front windows and wondered if the fall would kill her before the undead got to her. She doubted it. "Not ruling it out," she muttered. "I'm not going to die up here. I'm not going to be forever crawling through this dirt after I'm dead." Her fist pounded the floor. The din raised by the undead shoppers was almost overwhelming.

Painfully, Nikki crawled over to the small window. Her knees ached from crawling, and her hands still stung from the cuts. Rubbing the grime off the glass with her sleeve, she could see the low roof of the antique store next door. The moaning of the undead had subsided now. There was only the sound of things being bumped and knocked over.

"Do you bastards even know I am up here? If I leave, will you follow?" Her stomach rumbled painfully. "Die from hunger, or die from the fall. Make your choice, girl," Nikki grumbled. Slamming her fist on the floor, she roused the dead again. Using the noise for cover, she kicked at the glass. The first hit hurt her toes. She adjusted and kicked with the heel of her shoe. The glass shattered when it hit the concrete of the thin alley below. Every zombie in the street was drawn to the sound of the dead calling and the crashing.

"How the hell are you going to do this?" The cool air whipped her hair across her face. The alley was about four feet wide, and the other roof was three feet below her. She was weak and tired. Below, the alley was quickly filling with the dead. "OK, remember when we took gymnastics? We'll just…backflip to the other roof." She edged out of the window. Holding the broken frame, she positioned her feet to give her the best leverage. Her body hung out over the empty space between the buildings. She rocked somewhat to get some momentum. "Just like in the gym. Ready, one, two, three!"

She was in the air. She had meant to do a lovely, arching move that would land her gracefully on her feet. That had been the plan, anyway. Stars burst in front of her eyes, the breath left her body, and every inch burned with pain. Nikki had landed flat on her back on the roof. *Oh God, I'm paralyzed*, she thought through a haze. *No, I'm dead. I know it*. The first attempt to breathe was agony.

Coughing, she sputtered, "OK, not dead." Pain washed over her body. "Hurts too much to be paralyzed." She rolled onto her side. The first attempt to get upended in several minutes of lying still. Finally, on her feet, Nikki assessed the situation. "I'm on a roof. It's getting cold, and I still have nothing to eat or drink. This is so much better."

Beneath her feet, the tar-covered wood creaked. "Oh, fu—" Before the words had even left her mouth, she was in the air again. There was more pain as debris pelted her. This time, however, her landing wasn't as hard. A once-beautiful antique sofa of deep crimson velvet lay on splintered legs, the upholstery cushioning her fall. Her eyes focused on the hole above her. Hours later, she woke to light rain falling from the darkened opening.

The office held a desk, a mini-fridge, and a coatrack with a jacket. Warm water and stale Pop-Tarts had never been so delicious. About ten minutes after, the cramps doubled her over. Nikki learned to eat small bits after that and not to down the entire bottle. She lasted two days in the shop. Then the food was gone. She had found some clothes that weren't too old. It seemed the store did some consignment as well as the antiques. This she was thankful for; a clean shirt and jeans did wonders for how she felt.

A plan was half-formed in her mind. The street in front of this store was mostly empty. The undead seemed to still be interested in her last address. At night it might be easy to slip past them. Then it was just a few blocks over to the woods. Had to be fewer of them there; maybe she could find one of those hunting cabins. Those guys usually had food stocked up or something. Taking the last water bottle, a handful of silverware, and a fireplace poker, Nikki headed for the door.

Slowly and silently, she turned the deadbolt. The crack let in the cool air and the stink of death. Across the street, two of them didn't seem to notice the movement. Fighting the urge to run, she walked slowly down the street. At the corner she turned, heading toward the woods. She had caught the attention of one of the undead in the middle of the street. She quickened her pace, but the creature just kept watching her. Nikki drew level with it and passed by it. It seemed to lose interest. Nikki blew out the breath she was holding. A tear ran down her face. The little food she had eaten threatened to come up. At the next street, Nikki's resolve broke. The entire road was crowded with the undead.

It took all she had not to scream. Terrified tears ran down her face, and her legs threatened to drop her. Her breath came in bursts of panic, and dark tunnels formed in her vision. A moan rose from the crowd. The silverware flew out of her hand in the opposite direction from where she was running, its effectiveness lost in the clatter of the poker that dropped in sheer panic. Now she was running, brush and limbs scratching her face and the knees of her jeans wet from where she fell to the ground. She retched. Tears flowed freely, her breathing heavy and painful. She was tired of being tired and terrified.

Not What Was Expected

The excitement of the first few days was over. Kyle found that he really missed video games. He missed his music; he missed his escapes. Alistair's house had all the safety they could ever need, but it didn't have anything that he and his sister could enjoy. There were a few old board games, several movies, and books, but it was stuff their uncle liked. Even their parents didn't seem to enjoy it. Krissy made up games and played with Dude Cat, but she, too, got bored. She complained loudly when Kyle got to go outside and she didn't.

"You know, Dad," Kyle said on one of these expeditions, "it might not be a bad idea to show her how to use one of these." He waved the gun.

His father frowned at the gun. "I wouldn't even show you, but you already had one. I am not going to ask where you got it."

"I didn't have it before. I found it after all this started," Kyle immediately defended himself.

"Well, good, and I guess it's good you had it. And since you do, you're going to learn how to handle it properly." Ray fumbled with the safety on his own handgun. Kyle pushed the barrel away from his face.

"Jesus, Dad! You never point a gun at someone unless you intend to kill them." Kyle took the weapon. "First of all, this is the safety. You had it in the fire position. That should be on until you want to fire." He was shaking his head at his father. "OK, gun safety one-o-one." He pulled the magazine and checked the bullets. He cleared the chamber and flipped the safety back on. Handing the weapon back, he started his instructions. "OK, first we are going to learn how to load and ready the gun."

"Who is teaching who?" Ray asked, a small smile playing on his face. "Good God, don't let your mother know you know this much. How do you know this?"

"I've been kicking around the idea of joining the army. Thought it would come in handy."

In the Woods

"This is my zombie-free zone!" Nikki screamed, her eyes shut tight. Below her, she could hear them lumbering through the underbrush. They were coming through the darkness. One was already in view, shambling toward the tree she had climbed.

"When I open my eyes, they won't be there," she whispered. She shut her eyes tighter, her fists clenching and unclenching as she heard a low moan. A thud of a dead fist on the tree followed by limbs breaking told her the zombie was right below her. "When I open my eyes, they won't be there!" she shouted.

"Shhhh!"

Nikki grabbed tighter onto the tree, and her eyes flew open. Her head spun, looking in all directions. She only saw darkness. Straining her ears to hear the voice again, she only heard the dead shuffling below. Anger rose in her. She refused to look down. All she wanted to do was go home. She wished to be left alone. Ever since she had run out of the store, she had been followed. She could hear them moaning below her.

"Go *away!*" she cried.

"Shhhh!"

"Who's there?" she demanded. Her anger now directed at the voice on the breeze.

"Shhhh!" was the only reply apart from the moaning of the dead.

At the foot of the tree, she could hear their fingers clawing and scraping on the wood. Nikki could imagine bloody fingertips with nails breaking free and the obliviousness of the creatures. She had seen one fall over a rock; a compound fracture sent the bones in its arm through flesh and clothes. The zombie didn't even notice. One had spied her through a pair of trees. It had tried so hard to reach her that it nearly tore its own face off pushing through the rough bark.

"It's the wind in the trees, that is all," she said as she shut her eyes and began to repeat, "They won't be there when I open my eyes. They won't be there when I open my eyes—"

"Be quiet! Shhhh! They can hear you!" came a frantic whisper from her left—or was it right? Losing her grip for a second, she quickly clung back onto the tree. Balance regained, she swept the limbs aside, trying to locate the owner of the voice. All she saw as a squirrel several feet away, watching her. It seemed annoyed she was in its tree.

"Did you say that?" she asked the animal.

"If I say yes, will you be quiet?" the voice hissed from the blackness.

Again Nikki tried to find the source of the admonishment. Her head spun left and right in desperation. She wasn't sure if she actually heard someone or if the days without sleep were finally sending her over the edge. She desperately wanted to find the owner of the voice. Tears prickled at the corner of her eyes. There were zombies below her and a ghost voice with her in the tree. The first tear slid down her cheek.

"I want to go home," she whimpered.

"There is no one alive there," hissed the voice.

"I want them to go away." She sniffled, gesturing below her.

"If you are quiet, they will go away," the voice breathed.

She gave a little laugh and whispered, "If I'm quiet, they will leave. If I'm quiet, they will leave…" After a moment or two, she just thought it over and over in her head. It seemed to be working as she could no longer hear them below her. She began to relax. "If I'm quiet…"

"Uuuuuuuuuuhhhhhhhhhhhhhhh" rose from below; the call was joined by three additional tones—four zombies moaning for her, wanting her to join them.

"You said if I was quiet, they would go away!" she screamed. No answer came. "You used me to distract them!" Terror and anger fought for control. "You lied; they're still here. Make them go away!" she howled as tears of fear and fury ran down her face.

Crack…crack, crack…crack. Four blinding flashes and deafening blasts from right behind her head. Her ears rang. There was a muffled thud as someone jumped down from the tree. There was a high-pitched whine in her ear, mixed with all other sounds, which seemed a million miles away. Through the haze came a sound.

"There! I made them go away. But they never would have come if you had kept quiet," called an angry voice. Nikki felt as if she had a pillow over her head.

"Now get down here! We have to get moving. The sound will only bring their friends." She looked down right as the moon broke through the clouds. A shape was moving between the stilled bodies of the zombies. It was waving her down.

Carefully she began to slide down the tree. Her foot found the next branch, but her fingers and arms felt like rubber from holding on so tight. It wasn't her arms that gave out but a branch. A yelp of fright escaped her as the limb broke free. Her feet dangled in midair. Her fingers protested for a second; then she lost her grip and fell into strong arms.

"Shhhh," whispered the man who had caught her. She couldn't see his face behind his ski mask. She was scared of him. He was tall and dressed in dark camouflage. She was short and wearing a pink hooded sweatshirt with a jean jacket over it that she had found in the consignment shop. He set her on the ground and turned his back to her. Nikki felt the urge to run. Before she could take more than a step, he was facing her again.

He slung a heavy rifle over his shoulder. She looked at the darkness surrounding them. She could disappear fast in the darkness. She froze when he pulled out a large handgun and grabbed her hand. As he pulled her through the woods, Nikki was amazed at how little noise he made. She seemed to snap every twig as every dried leaf that ever seemed to have fallen crunched underfoot. Every noise she made felt as if it were amplified a thousand times, advertising their location to the zombies.

"At least my hearing is coming back," she muttered and was quickly shushed.

As she was pulled through the trees, her heart was pounding and her lungs were on fire. She regretted not trying harder in gym class. Something lunged forward out of the dark at them. The muzzle flashed, and her ears rang again as the man fired at the zombie. Nikki swore—her ears really hurt now.

The crumpled form of the zombie lay across their path. She was pulled along as her companion began to inspect it. Nikki pulled back, trying not to get close as the man flipped over the corpse and began to search it. He patted the filthy jacket of the creature, letting go of Nikki's hand as he rummaged in the pockets. Standing up, he held up a gun that caught the moonlight on its polished barrel.

Her hand free, Nikki began to back away. Ready to sprint, she turned. In a flash he had her by the wrist, pulling her closer to the zombie.

"I don't—" she began, but he cut her off.

"Shhhh," he warned as he handed her the gun. He stuffed a box that rattled into her jacket pocket. She then felt a cold knife hilt pressed into her hand. She stared down at the gun, felt the ammo box press against her stomach, and held the knife that was in a sheath. Perplexed, she looked into the eyes in the ski mask and opened her mouth. He shook his head. He took the knife and attached it to the waist of her jeans. He checked the gun; it was empty. He reached in her pocket and retrieved the ammo box, shook out some bullets, loaded the gun, and flipped off the safety.

Pressing the weapon back into her hand, he made a gun with his thumb and finger and gestured the gun firing. He flipped the safety back on and made his fingers like a gun but then nothing when he did the "bang-bang." He gestured at her to see if she understood.

She glared at him and rolled her eyes. With a mouth-open nod, she mouthed in a "duh" manner. The eyes in the mask rolled. He turned and started to move across a field. She gave him the finger and looked at the gun and then into the woods.

Safety in numbers, she thought and began to follow him. She was just catching up to him when he threw an arm out to stop her.

In the Cabin

The arm stayed across her path, but Nikki wasn't going anywhere. She saw it, too—a light up ahead. It wasn't moving. She looked at him; he stared back. She pointed at the light and held her hands up. He shrugged and inclined his head toward the light. She shrugged and raised her eyebrows. He let out a little laugh.

"Shhhh," she replied and heard him fight to keep from laughing. He motioned with his head again, and they set off toward the light. As they crept along slowly, the outline of a small building became clear. It looked like a hunting cabin, the type Nikki had thought about escaping to. Excitement bloomed in her. She didn't care how musty the sheets would be, how lumpy the mattress, or how thin the cot. It was someplace to sleep, maybe get some food in her stomach.

They had arrived at the edge of a clearing. The cabin sat in the middle of it. Nikki's companion motioned for her to get down. She crouched next to him. Looking over, she saw he was intently watching the cabin. She tapped him on the shoulder and held up her hands. He made binoculars with his hands on his eyes and pointed at the window. She gestured a "Yeah, and?" He held up one finger, telling her to wait. Together they watched the window. Nothing happened. Again she raised her hands in a "Well?" He flexed his fists, rolled his eyes, pointed to her, and waved her on. She frowned at him and shooed him forward. He pumped his fists in frustration, beckoned her to follow, and began to cross the clearing.

They approached the small cabin slowly and crouched over. A light blazed in a window set high, near the roof. All the windows on the ground level were boarded up. A ladder lay on the ground under the window with the light in it. Holding up a hand telling her to wait, her silent companion crept over to the front door. He tried it; nothing happened. It was bolted tight.

Returning to her side, he shrugged and then bent over to retrieve the ladder. He lifted it into position and laid it as gently as he could against the house. Next, he motioned for her to climb. She shook her head no and motioned for him to go first. He raised his shoulders and motioned again.

"What if one of them is up there?" she hissed.

Growling in response he pointed at her. He held the ladder. He pointed at himself and motioned climbing. Halfway through his pantomime, she was waving him on hurriedly. A noise in the darkness made the interior that much more inviting. While she was second-guessing if she really did want to go first, her decision was made as her hand was thrust onto the side of the ladder. It was held there, the eyes in the mask boring into hers.

"Yeah, yeah," she whispered again, indicating to him to hurry. Brows furrowed under the knitted eyeholes. A grumble sounding like "shuddalefter" disappeared in the noise of the ladder scraping down slightly as the feet sank into the soft earth.

Even in this, his movements were quiet. He was at the top, crouching just below the window. Slowly he inched up to peer through the window. He stood up completely, checking out the area as far as he could. Nikki cringed when he tapped on the glass and returned to his crouch. The ladder shook; she tightened her grip. He whistled down. She watched as he gestured that he couldn't see any movement in the room. He was standing again and trying the window. It opened easily, and he slipped through. Nikki's foot was on the bottom rung when his head appeared out the window. He motioned for her to wait. A deep frown crossed her face. Now that she was alone, the darkness seemed to creep ever closer. Her hearing was returning slowly, yet every sound seemed amplified a hundredfold. Her hands gripped the ladder as she nervously tried to see any movement from the shadows. Every rustle of dry leaves and every animal noise screamed an approaching zombie.

"Come on, come on, where are you?" she whispered. A horrible thought crossed her mind: *What if he found one, and it got him?* Her attention returned to the light above. Terrified that she was alone again, she started to back away from the cabin, keeping the window in sight. Her breath exhaled in a rush of relief when his head poked out the window again.

"Psst," he hissed, motioning for her to come up. She was on the ladder and halfway up in seconds. Something was moving in the trees. Glancing up she could see he was watching something else, not her, as he held the ladder steady. She paused, looking back over her shoulder. "Come on, hurry it up," he hissed. His order, mixed with the crunching of the bushes, urged her to the opening.

Shaking with fear and exertion, she allowed him to grab her arms. "What took so long?" she demanded as she began to climb through.

"Had to make sure it was clear," he grumbled as he helped her through the window. Once she was in, he knocked over the ladder.

"How are we supposed to get out if we need to?" she asked, exasperated. The mistrust began to return to her stomach. Her hand found the hilt of the knife.

"Through the front door," he replied, ignoring her reach. He pulled off the ski mask. He was older than she was but not much, maybe twenty or so.

"Then why did you make me climb the ladder?"

"Huh?" he grunted while rubbing his hands through his mussed hair and scratching his chin. He started to walk away. She stood dumbfounded and watched him go, shaking her head at him.

"Brilliant. I'm stuck with an idiot," she mumbled.

"OK. So where is the body?" she asked with more bravery than she felt. She began to inspect the room. There was no sign of a struggle, no blood on the floor or walls.

"What body?" he asked, inspecting the lamp. It was a battery-operated one, very bright.

"Well, there is no one here, so I assume they are dead. Why else would the place be empty?" She glared at him, her hands on her hips.

"Don't know." He shrugged.

"Did you check the cellar? They are always in the cellar," she said, her brave tone wavering.

"Nah, just up here."

She started to panic and head to the stairs. "So they could be below us right now?" Fear drove her voice up an octave. She was torn between the window and the stairs. All she wanted to do was get out. She was positive the cellar would be teeming with zombies all ready to spill out and get her, or perhaps there was a sea of them milling about in front of the door. Her only escape route was blocked because this dolt knocked over the ladder. She had been having nightmares like this since the first night.

Picking up the battery-powered lantern that was lighting the room, he walked over to her. "My name is Shane, and I will not let them get you. What is your name?"

"What? We have to get out of here. I know we do." She was heading toward full-on panic now.

"Hey, it's cool. The downstairs is clean; there is no cellar. I don't know where the owner went or when they will be back, or your name," he tried to reassure her.

"You said you didn't go downstairs! What if they come back and kill us for breaking into the house? What if they bring them back with them? Then we'll be surrounded, and—and..."

"I went down the stairs and could see most of the rooms," Shane soothed. "Shhhh..."

"What?" she hissed and dropped to a crouch. "Do you hear something?"

"No, I was trying to calm you down." He laughed.

"Oh, this is funny?" she demanded. "You've brought us into the house of death!"

"No, but you are." He was smiling at her. "Damn, jumpy, you need to relax—house of death."

She glared at him. "Nikki," she huffed.

"Hi, Nikki." He held out his hand and added, "Can I call you Nik?"

She glared at it for a second and then shook it. "No," she replied.

"Whatever." He shrugged, letting go of her hand. He grabbed the lantern as he headed down the stairs. Darkness enveloped her for a moment. Fear welled up, and she hurried after him.

At the bottom of the stairs, she found herself in a small living room with a fireplace; to her left was a small kitchen. A door stood to the right. She hissed at Shane and pointed to the door.

"It is truly scary in there," he whispered. "A horrible sight."

She backed away, hiding behind him; her voice cracked as her hand gripped his arm tightly. "Blood? Body parts? Body?"

"Shitter." He guffawed and received a painful punch in the arm for his joke. He tried to act as if it didn't hurt. Rubbing the area, he decided not to mess with her too much right now. He also began to second-guess the wisdom of giving her that knife.

Shane began to build a fire, so Nikki curled up on the couch. Pulling an old afghan off the back of a lumpy piece of furniture, she wrapped it around herself, not caring that it smelled musty. The fire crackled and spread warmth through the room.

She didn't realize how tired she was until she woke with a start. For a second she didn't know where she was. Then it all came back, and the hope that was always there when she woke was gone—the hope that it had all been a terrible dream. When she had been hiding in the attic for those days—weeks?—she really had no idea how long, but when she would wake, she would lie there for a moment with her eyes closed. She would try to ignore that she was not in her bed, and for just that moment, she would think, W*hen I open my eyes, I'll be in my bed, and none of it will have happened.* But then she did open her eyes, and she would be staring up at the rafters and know it all had.

Rolling onto her side, she looked over at Shane. She watched him for a few moments and wondered what he was thinking. He was staring into the fire. Occasionally he would poke at the coals, causing the log to spark. There seemed no other point to his ministrations to the fire. They had been in the cabin for a couple of hours and hadn't spoken more since he had told her where the bathroom was. Her hand found the hilt of the knife; the gun he had given her was lying on the floor within reach. As she watched him, she couldn't help but wonder at his intentions. She was very grateful to him for dispatching the undead and for helping her, but he made her nervous. He looked as if he had been living outside for a while, judging by his unkempt, matted hair, scruffy beard, and filthy clothes. She had only been forced out of her hiding place two days ago.

"So what's the plan?" she asked. She grimaced at the startled jump from him, as if he had forgotten she was there.

"Well, I think we should rest up here for a while…get cleaned up." He looked down at himself. "Been a while for me."

She decided not to comment.

"Then," he continued without looking at her, "I was heading to my uncle Alistair's. He is a survival nut and has this bunker thing that is all decked out for the end of the world…So that seems like the place to be." Shane poked the fire again. "You can come along if you want."

"Thanks," Nikki responded, but the thought made her a little uneasy. Two guys in a bunker and her—that sounded like a safe bet. "I'll think about it."

As if hearing her concern, Shane added, "Uncle Alistair's wife Rebecca is really cool. She'd love to have another woman around to talk to."

A wife, huh? Well, this sounded a little better. "So where are they?" She decided to see what Shane was like and would make a decision based on him.

"Next county over. They got this place next to the mountain. Backs right up to it so you can't get to the house from the back unless you rappel down to it." He was absentmindedly scratching his beard. "It is surrounded by, like, a ten-foot-high wall that has razor wire on top. The wall is two feet thick and has this crazy metal gate that retracts into the front wall." He closed his eyes, trying to remember the details. "About every twenty feet out from the main wall are fences, all the way out to the main road." Shane got more excited the more he spoke.

"Wow, how did the hell could anyone afford all that?" Nikki couldn't help but ask. A house built into a mountain had to be really expensive.

"Oh, Uncle Alistair made a lot of money on real estate or something. Dad never told me." Shane jabbed the fire and was quiet for a moment. "Well, Uncle Alistair has lots of money and is really paranoid. So he built the compound. It has solar power, wind power, rain collection, and a well. He has a generator with something like ten years of fuel and more weapons than you can imagine. Some of them I don't think are legal, but like I said, he has money." Shane turned to look at Nikki. "Got to be safer than this place, right?" Then he laughed. "Maybe he was in the mob or an assassin or something."

She just smiled and nodded. "Or something. Do you want to get some sleep? I'll watch the fire for a bit."

"I'm OK for now; you go back to sleep. I'll wake you when I need to," he assured her.

Nikki closed her eyes and drifted back off to sleep. Her dreams now had her fighting a zombie horde from the stone walls of a castle. This was a good dream. A beam of sunlight from a crack in the boarded-up window woke her, and for a moment she panicked. Shane was not in the room, but then she heard him in the kitchen.

"Didn't you get any sleep?" she asked, stretching her sore back. It was better than the trees she had been sleeping in, but the couch was still quite lumpy.

"No, but now that you're up, we'll grab a bite, and I'll sack out for a few. I've taken to sleeping during the day." He walked over and handed her some stale bread with jam on it. "Not much else here. Doesn't look like we'll stay too long."

She nodded her thanks. "Maybe that is why the last person left?" she mused. He shrugged and finished his bread and sat down on the chair next to her.

"Wait, hey, take the couch," she said, jumping up.

Shaking his head, he waved her down. "No thanks, I prefer to be in a more upright position." He slumped into the chair, dropped his feet onto a low footstool, put his head back, and closed his eyes. It was only a few moments before his breathing took on the steady pace of sleep. She noticed that he kept the rifle barrel in his hand as he slept.

How long have you been out here? she thought while studying his face. There were dark circles under his eyes and scratches on his face. The ghost of a bruise was still on his cheek. His hands also bore the signs of being outdoors for a while. She noticed he had washed them, but that only caused the cuts and scratches to show more vividly. Had he been alone from the start? If not, what happened to the others? Did he leave them to die, and she was just the bait if he got into trouble later? She was on her feet now, moving a little closer as if looking at his sleeping face would betray his intent. *OK, Nikki, knock it off. He may just be a good guy.* She returned to the couch.

She didn't want to be alone, but sitting in the living room was really boring. She got up and wandered around the room, being as quiet as possible. The room was dimly lit, with only cracks of light making it through the barricades. There were no books or magazines, nothing to distract her brain. So she kept going into the dark place in her mind that always found the worst possibilities. Shaking the thought that she was being kept alive as a food source, she made her way to one of the boarded-up windows and looked through an opening.

It was a brilliantly sunny morning. She could feel the cold through the glass as a draft blew across her face. *One of the windows had to be broken*, she thought. As she stepped back to find the opening, her foot slipped on what she thought were several small stones until the tinkle of metal told her differently. As she bent down to get a better look, her eyes readjusted to the gloom. It wasn't stones but shell casings. That feeling of dread crept back into her chest. Now that she was looking for it, she could see that all around the wall, there were lots of brass casings. Someone had been shooting—and shooting a lot.

"OK, so where did they go?" she whispered. She was not sure if waking Shane would be a good idea; his hand twitched on the rifle. Nikki made her way to the stairs and looked back into the room. Shane's head rolled to the side as he gave a loud snort and shuffled on the chair. He was still sleeping. She surveyed the scene for a moment. The windows were boarded tight, the door securely barred. Why was the place empty? She nervously fingered the knife on her hip and reached inside her jacket to feel the hilt of the gun.

"OK, Nik, you're still armed, and Shane seems to know what he is doing. Let's have a look upstairs. You know there is nothing up there," she whispered to herself while staring up the stairs. A full minute passed with her foot still on the bottom step.

"Come on, girl, get it together," she huffed. Shane grunted from the chair. She pulled the gun from her jacket and mounted the stairs. Slowly and carefully she advanced, pausing to cringe on a creaky stair. Nothing happened; Shane didn't even grunt. Blowing out the breath she'd been holding, she continued on.

Halfway up the stairs, she began to notice scratches on the stairs and walls. They looked like someone's fingernails had clawed at the wood. Near the top, she noticed blood in the scratches. At the top of the stairs was a stain she hadn't noticed the night before. It was dried blood. It was a large pool, but it seemed thin as if it had been cleaned. Something else odd about it was that there was a right-angle cutting into the pool.

There must have been a rug, but where did it go? Nikki thought as the pit of her stomach tightened. The upstairs was one room. There was a bed along the one wall and a dresser by the window. Other than this, there was nothing except..."The closet," she whispered.

Silently she crept up to the door. A shaking hand reached out to the doorknob. It squeaked as she slowly turned it. The latch slipped free, and she flung the door open, gun poised and ready.

"Oh...God!" she gasped. "Who the hell owns this much flannel?" Relief crashed over her; the gun hung slack in her hand at her side. The bottom of the closet was empty except for a pair of muddy boots. She grabbed one of the less-offensive-looking flannels and pulled it over her jacket and headed to the window. More confused than ever, she whispered, "Under the bed..." Head-turning slowly, she began to crouch down. "Ugh..." Her face crinkled in disgust as she only saw crumpled tissues. Rolling her shoulders to relieve the tension of the last few minutes, she wandered closer to the window.

"Someone died here, but where did they go? If someone survived, so where did they go?" she pondered. Something caught her eye. Several long, black hairs swayed in the cold breeze. They were caught in the rough wood of the window frame. They were too long and too dark to be Nikki's. "Were you coming or going through the window?" she asked the hairs.

When You're Downtown

Mary and Chris spent the first day away from the others in the apartment. The woman who let them in was older; she reminded Mary of a teacher. Her name was Gwen. Another woman there was only a few years older; she had short, spiky hair, blond that turned orange and then red as it progressed, giving her the appearance of flame. Her name was Hayley. Chris learned that Hayley and Gwen had worked together somewhere. Gwen had been the manager and Hayley her assistant. They carried over this relationship to how they ran the apartment.

So along with those two, there were four other people in the apartment: a couple in their thirties, an older man, and another woman who was older but not as old as the man, as far as Mary could tell. The group stayed together, cramped into the one-bedroom studio apartment for three days. Nobody knew whose place it was. From what Mary had gathered, Gwen and Hayley had met the older man on the first floor. Together they were hiding. They picked up the other woman and her daughter the first night. The five of them had explored the second floor, finding several zombies. That was where they had lost the daughter. The third floor was clear, so they found the open apartment and made it their safe place.

After the fourth day, the young couple left to find relatives. Gwen had tried to talk them out of it. The older man, Mary couldn't remember his name, had not bothered much to dissuade them. His comment was "The food will last longer."

"I wanna go, too," Mary whispered to Chris after the couple left. She trusted Gwen and Hayley, but the other two bothered her. The man was always watching her. It made her uncomfortable. Hayley had noticed and had already started hovering around her. This also bothered Mary. The other woman—Sue was her name—was always crying. Mary felt bad for her, but it only went so far. Mary and Chris had lost their parents and friends. "Everyone has lost someone," Mary grumbled in Chris's ear. "Get over it and move on. We needed to think about what's next. How are we going to get out of this mess? We can't stay in town." Chris hushed her as the conversation began to heat.

"We haven't seen any of them for two days," Mr. Creepy, as Mary referred to him, argued.

"No, but we don't know where they were going," Gwen countered. "It might have been across town or even the next town over. We still have a lot of food here," she continued.

"Plus the Davises said they'd send help as soon as they could," Hayley offered.

"That was how long ago? They are dead. No one is coming! We are on our own," Creepy said, his volume increasing with each sentence.

Hayley spoke up again. "Sue, Chris, Mary, what are your opinions?" Creepy began to protest about children but was silenced by Hayley's anger. "Young, old, doesn't matter! We are all in this together, and we will make decisions that way!"

Gwen stepped between the two, hands raised and voice calm. "This is not a prison." She turned to face Hayley. "And it is not a democracy." Now Gwen was addressing everyone. "We have food and shelter here. You are free to leave at any time." Creepy began to stuff things into a bag. "However, you will not take what does not belong to you, and you will not take more than you need."

The man turned to her, his face a tangle of angry scowling. "What do you mean?"

"I mean," Gwen snagged a box of cereal he held, "you are welcome to a share of what we have, but you will not take all of anything."

Mary watched as he went from creepy to murderous. Stepping forward to snatch back the food, he was stopped by the click-clack of a weapon being cocked. Chris nudged Mary, inclining his head toward the gun held at Hayley's side. Gwen's eyes bulged at the sight. Sue whimpered, scampering onto the lumpy sofa and curling into a ball.

"What are you gonna do? Shoot me over some Kiddy Crunch?"

"If I have to." Hayley's hand shook, but her eyes held a steely gaze. "You want to leave, then go. If you all want to leave, we'll divvy up the goods and part ways. I am staying here."

"With the gun, no doubt," Creepy growled.

Gwen stood facing Hayley. "Where did you get that?"

"From a gun store after my ex-boyfriend couldn't seem to let go." Hayley's glare never left the man's face. "And don't worry, it turns out I'm a pretty good shot."

Something Wicked

Nikki watched the strands float in the breeze until something else caught her attention. Out of the corner of her eye, she saw movement by the tree line. Then it struck her that the tree line used to be closer. The area around the house had been cleared recently, but very haphazardly. It was as if whoever did it got bored or interrupted halfway through. "You'd think they would have done a nicer job," she mumbled.

"I might not have done a good job either if zombies were attacking," Shane said, sending her heart through her chest as her feet left the ground.

"Don't do that!" she shouted, rubbing her chest. Calming slightly, she glared at him. "When did you get up?"

"Just now." He moved closer to the window. "And you shouldn't wander off." Shane stared past her out to the tree line. She rolled her eyes at him.

"You sound like my dad," she grumbled.

"You act like my sister, and that didn't end well," he stated as he turned to face her. "Don't wander off." She began to protest, but the look on his face told her now was not the time. He brushed past her and headed to the closet.

"Nothing in there but a bunch of flannel," she stated while looking back at the tree line, wondering what happened to his sister, even if she felt she already knew.

Shane's back was to her as he moved the shirts around, taking out one and then two. He held the boots up to his feet. They were too big for him. He ran his hand over the top shelf and found nothing but dust. He clapped his hands together, sending it cascading through the room.

Nikki turned as she sneezed. "Oh shit," she whispered as one of the undead stumbled out of the woods. Shane was at her side in an instant.

"We are OK; he can't get to us," he assured her, but as he did so, another one came out of the woods. She sucked in a breath and began to back away from the window as a third emerged.

"OK, not good, time to go." Nikki was backing away from the window and heading toward the stairs.

Shane mirrored her but kept saying, "We're fine; they can't get to us." But his tone betrayed his concern.

"Are you trying to convince me, you, or them?" Nikki tried to joke through a trembling voice.

"Yes," he replied as the fourth zombie stumbled out of the brush. As if on cue, they all stopped. So did Shane and Nikki. The zombies looked confused. They stumbled around in circles; a zombie in a business suit fell over a log. Nikki gave a little laugh and immediately felt ashamed. It didn't last long. Her hand clenched tightly on Shane's arm as the undead began to howl. The color drained from his face, yet he still patted her hand reassuringly. Shane edged forward, Nikki firmly attached to his arm but behind him. Looking out of the window, he saw the group turn and head back into the woods. They moved with a purpose, moving faster than their normal mindless shuffle.

"They found someone," Shane whispered. "This was just a potential. They actually found someone."

"What do you mean?" Nikki whimpered.

"I mean, they were just wandering to the house. They heard something, and you saw how they moved; they were…" But what they were doing was left hanging in the room, as several gunshots were heard.

Nikki increased her grip on Shane's arm. "Let's go while they are distracted," she exclaimed while trying to pull him to the stairs.

Shane stood still for a moment, ignoring her insistence. Something in the woods troubled him. "Yeah, yeah, maybe you're right," he finally said. Turning quickly, he pulled his arm free and then hurried toward the stairs, leaving Nikki to stare, shocked, at his departure.

Regaining her thoughts, she exclaimed, "Hey, wait!" Running after him, she took the stairs two at a time. Behind her through the window, a lone figure emerged from the woods, with a heavy bag over his shoulder.

Back to the Woods

Shane was quickly collecting his things from the living room; his bag was slung over his shoulder, and the rifle was cradled in his arms by the time Nikki hit the bottom of the stairs. He held a finger to his lips as he motioned her to get to the door. She didn't question him but just helped move the heavy bar from across the door. She hurried forward and unbolted the deadbolt. Her hand moved to the handle, but his hand flew up, motioning for her to wait. He pointed to himself and then to her. She pulled the gun out from inside her jacket and nodded her readiness. He gave her a look. "What?" she mouthed.

"Safety," he hissed.

She took a moment to figure it out. It clicked off, and Shane moved the barrel far away from him. He nodded to her; she returned it. Both took a deep breath. Shane flung open the door. Nikki's hands shook. Quickly Shane moved around the door to look out onto the porch.

It was clear. Checking the surrounding area, he motioned for Nikki to follow. The cold air greeted them in the early-morning sun. It again dazzled her as she shielded her eyes after the gloom of the cabin. Shane had barely taken three steps off the porch when they heard it.

"Well, hello there," a gruff voice called. "I don't remember having guests."

Slowly Nikki and Shane turned to the source of the voice. Shane was careful not to appear threatening. He lowered his rifle but did not take his finger away from the trigger. A man who appeared to be in his late fifties or sixties was approaching the cabin. He had unkempt white hair and a scruffy beard. He was wearing a pair of filthy jeans, boots, and a flannel shirt under a grubby orange vest jacket. He was carrying a large bag that he let drop when he reached the end of the porch.

"I see you made yerselves at home," the man said as he adjusted his rifle into a more readied position.

"Yeah, sorry about that," Shane said. "Didn't think anyone lived here."

"No, I can see that a bolted door and a lantern burning would give the impression of tha place a-being empty." The man gave a humorless laugh.

"Yeah, well, we are leaving; so sorry about staying in your house," Shane said while backing away, pushing Nikki behind him. He had his own gun ready.

"She ain't going nowhere in my shirt." The old man referenced Nikki with his rifle.

"Right! Sorry," she said, quickly stripping off the flannel, holding it out.

"There, no harm. So we'll just be leaving," Shane stated. "Just leave it there." He turned his head slightly to address Nikki while not letting his eyes leave the newcomer. Nikki laid the shirt down, keeping her gun hidden behind Shane.

The old man's eyes only darted back to Shane for a second as he leered at Nikki. He made her increasingly uncomfortable. His tongue darted out through the beard. "Well, you can go, boy, but I think *you* can stay." He readjusted the gun again to point at Shane. "Consider it rent. Now go on, boy, get."

Shane's rifle was up and pointed at the man. "Let's call this a misunderstanding and head our separate ways. There is enough dead wandering around. You don't need to be one of them." As he spoke Shane put some distance between them, backing up and pushing Nikki further along the porch.

Nikki's left foot met air as they reached the end of the porch. Instinctively her hands grabbed Shane's arm. She was falling backward, pulling him along with her. Shane's gun left its mark to point at the ceiling of the porch. At once Nikki screamed, the man's gun fired, and Shane howled, falling beside her.

Nikki rolled over and sat up. She tried to pull the trigger on her gun. Nothing happened. Shane had dropped his rifle in the fall. Wood on the post next to his head splintered as the man fired a second round at him. The third shot clicked; panic showed in the eyes of the shooter as he tried to clear the round.

"Safety!" Shane screamed at Nikki. She had put it back on when they seemed safe.

"Where?" she shouted back, cursing herself for putting it back on.

"On the gun, you…" Shane cried, jumping to his feet. He ran full force at the man as he cleared the misfire. He slammed a round home. The gun boomed, and wood splintered off the wall close to Nikki. Shards of shattered wood flew, cutting into her face and hand. The heavy gun clattered on the boards. Shane's shoulder slammed into the shooter, sending them both to the ground.

Nikki scrambled to her feet. Ignoring the sting on her face, she ran over to the struggle. Finally flipping off the safety, she swore loudly. She couldn't get a clear shot. Shane was on top, punching every inch he could get to. Suddenly Shane was flipped over. The silver gleam of a blade flashed. Shane threw up his arm to block the blow. They rolled; Nikki's target disappeared. Screaming in frustration, Nikki dropped the revolver and snatched up the knife from her waist.

Shane was on the bottom again, and the man was pushing down with all his weight, the blade getting ever closer to Shane's throat. With a cry, Nikki flew into the melee. A howl of agony erupted when Nikki plunged the blade of her knife into Shane's attacker's back.

In a flash the man's arms flew out, smashing the hilt of his knife into her temple. Stars exploded behind her eyes; pain filled her head. She was on her back, the base of her skull bouncing off the planks of the porch. Suddenly, through the fog that was her mind, her ears were ringing with a hideous howl. She rolled over, trying to regain her feet. As she made it to her hands and knees, she was grabbed roughly. Crying out, she tried to fight. An arm snaked across her chest, and the other was across her stomach and wrenched her to her feet.

"Stop fighting! Come on!" Shane screamed into her dazed face. "Nik, move!" He dropped her on her feet. She stumbled and fell. Again Shane pulled her to her feet. Suddenly he leaned heavily on her. She could barely hold her own weight, let alone his. The cabin door slammed closed. There was more gunfire. Nikki couldn't tell where it was coming from. "We have to move," Shane groaned.

Her eyes began to focus, and she could see a group of zombies shuffling fast across the open space from the woods to the cabin. The pain in her head screamed as she stood up straight, fighting the urge to vomit. Shane was heavy against her. She realized he was hurt. She wasn't sure how bad, but she was sure it was bad enough. Her vision was still blurry, and her balance was bad.

"You have to guide." Nikki huffed as she fought to keep the bile and stale bread from coming up. Together they limped as fast as they could away from the zombies and the cabin. Her vision began to clear with her balance returning. Nearing the woods, she turned to look back. The scene stopped her in horror; Shane fell as she did. "Oh God, are those hands?" she cried. Half of the cabin's roof was shingled in the leathered, severed hands of the dead.

Shane grabbed her arm, pulling himself to his feet. Ignoring the gruesome display, he pulled her forward. "Come on," he wheezed. She got under his arm; again they were moving. Her astonished cry had not gone unnoticed. Two of the dead had heard them breaking off from the main group surrounding the cabin, and they were pursuing them. Reaching the woods, they were able to outmaneuver the zombies for a while. Shane became heavier and slower until Nikki could barely support him.

As they hid behind a couple of large trees, Shane motioned for Nikki to shoot the closest undead. With a nod, she began to search her jacket. It was then she remembered dropping it back at the cabin. Raising her arms, she noted no gun to Shane. "Shit," he whispered, checking his own jacket. His rifle was also back at the cabin. He made stabbing motions, telling her to use her knife.

"It's still in that crazy dude," she hissed.

Slumping against the tree, Shane rechecked his jacket. His hand paused for a second and then dipped inside. A weak smile crossed his face as he pulled out another handgun. His face was pale. He was sweating badly, and his breathing was labored. He used the tree to hold himself up.

Nikki noticed blood seeping through his shirt, the stain growing by the second. She saw the knee of his jeans was also torn and bloody. She ran a hand through her hair in fear. He was hurt really bad. She let her hand drop and noticed it came back crimson. The throb returned. Distracted by her own injuries, she jumped as two shots boomed nearby, felling the pursuing zombies.

"Come on, the sound might bring more," he wheezed, trying to push himself off the tree.

"How bad is it?" she asked, getting under his arm to steady him.

"Hurts like a fucker. How's your head?" He tried to smile, reaching up to brush her hair aside to look. Halfway up he faltered; with a groan, he let his arm fall to his side.

"Shane, we need to find a place to rest." She looked around. Not seeing anything but trees, she began to move forward.

"Ow, oh God," he moaned. She immediately stopped, concerned. He looked over at her. "Sorry, just a blinding case of the obvious." He coughed as he tried to laugh.

"When you are feeling better, I'm going to beat your ass," she grumbled. He tried to laugh again as she pulled him further into the woods. They could still hear the gunfire from the cabin.

Unwanted Company

Even though it was a nice day outside, Ray was uncomfortable with Krissy going out. He and Kyle had cleaned out the yard and closed off the front gate with the second set of metal doors. This did not, however, keep out the smell or the sound. Jen thought it would be good to let Krissy run around and get some exercise.

"Come on, man," Kyle complained. "Let her get out for a bit. She is driving me crazy."

"You're not the only one...Dude," Ray replied. "All right, but we are going to be out there with her." Once outside, Ray immediately regretted the decision. He had forgotten the propensity of his daughter to scream for no reason. Kyle had been playing tag with her, and she had been laughing and screeching until the moaning drowned out everything else.

Jen had ushered them all back into the house. "Alistair says the...things are agitated for a couple of blocks around us," Kyle swore under his breath. "Kyle, don't swear," his mother admonished and then sighed. "But, yes, that about sums up things." Kyle tried not to laugh until he saw the screen behind his mother. He had seen videos of Mecca and the devote circling it. The zombies surrounding their fortress looked similar. Five or six thick, close to the walls, with more moving in every moment, the zombies seemed to be a swarm.

"What happens if they start to climb over each other?" Kyle asked the monitor.

"Fortunately, I don't think that will happen too soon. Our bigger problem is going to be them building up a ramp." Ray pointed to the group closest to the wall. They were raised slightly above the others. The wall itself was covered in gore. The pressure of the outer rings of the undead on the inner was grinding the corpses up. Kyle could imagine bodies trampled underfoot in an ever-growing pile.

"I didn't think there was that many people in this town," Kyle whispered.

"What are you watching?" Krissy demanded.

"Nothing, just boring stuff." Jen smiled. Kyle frowned at her. Ray gave a slight nod to his son.

"Krissy, we were just looking outside the walls," Kyle began. Jen hissed him quiet. He ignored her. "There are a lot of the bad people around us." Jen was appealing to her husband for help. Ray shook his head.

"I think she should know," he told his wife.

"Mom, I know we are trapped. I know the bad, dead people want to hurt us." Krissy spoke with her hands on her hips. "I'm not a baby or stupid, you know."

"No, sis, you aren't." Kyle smiled.

"Besides, if it gets bad, Uncle Alistair will come to get us. He has a castle that we will be able to stay in until it is safe outside again," Krissy finished. She spotted Dude Cat and took off after him.

"Seems we don't have to worry about scaring her with the truth." Jen sighed.

"Better to be straight with her. She needs to know the danger," Kyle said. A hand appeared on his shoulder.

"Slowly," his father whispered in his ear. Kyle knew that what he meant was his mother wasn't ready for Krissy to be exposed to what the world was now. Kyle thought to let her think there was a safe place was worse than the truth.

A Place to Rest

They had traveled for about an hour, and Nikki was exhausted. Shane was becoming heavier and slower with every step. Finding a large log, she eased him down so he could rest against it. The groan escaping his throat frightened her. Was he becoming one of them? Would his groan call to them? How would she protect them if it did? Could she kill him if he turned? All these thoughts fought for dominance as she pulled her hand from around his waist. Looking at it, she was horror-struck as it dripped with blood.

"Oh God, we need to get that stopped or you're going to bleed to death," she whispered.

As he looked up at her, a smile weakly spread across his face. She was struck by how extremely pale he was. His face was cold to the touch, and his lips and the area around his eyes were a deep gray. If she hadn't been with him, she would have mistaken him for one of the walking undead. He tried to lift his arm but let it fall to the ground. He tried again to point to something behind her. It was more of a vague wave. She turned and looked up. A covered platform was attached to a large tree.

"What is it?" she asked.

"Treestand," he answered, his voice barely audible. "Safety."

"Got it, so up we go." She began to pull him to his feet.

"No…you…go." His eyes were unfocused. He tried to push her away.

"Save what you got left for the climb. I can't carry you." She had him on his feet. Half carrying, half dragging, she got him to the base of the tree. "OK, I'm going up; maybe there is a rope or something I can haul your sorry ass up with." It was difficult getting up to the stand. She was not much of an outdoors person, and her legs reminded her of this fact. To her surprise, there was a moldy-looking length of rope coiled under a small tarp. She tied off the end and scrambled back down to Shane. He was already attempting to make the climb as she tied the rope around him. She hurried back up the stand, spurred on by the moaning and rustling of the woods. Her hands ached and her muscles burned when Shane was finally lying next to her on the platform. Shane rolled onto his back and groaned, "Hope this holds us." He laughed, but it turned into a cough. "Should have left me."

"You're probably right," she said, trying to distract from what she was about to do. Pulling his shirt up, she fought the urge to be sick. The blood-drenched fabric stuck to the wound. From what she could see through the thick crimson, there was a small hole in his side. It gushed out blood every time he breathed. Taking a few deep breaths and then exhaling slowly, she asked, "Do you have anything to stop the bleeding?"

Shane nodded while trying to reach into one of his pockets. She moved his hand and did it for him. The only thing she found was a long lock-blade knife. Closed, it was about five inches long. He weakly pushed it to her.

"It was my sister's," he mumbled.

"Shh," she said, putting the knife down and searching her own pockets. "I don't need to open you up any further. I need to stop the bleeding." Her hand found some cloth, which she pulled from the inside. It was an old padded bra she had taken from the thrift shop. "Well, at least they are clean. I hope you appreciate this," she said as she took the knife and cut out the cups. "This is the last clean thing I own."

Shane gave a weak smile and then groaned as she pushed the garment onto the wound. Holding pressure as she had always seen in movies, she watched Shane's face. He was semiconscious. After a while, the bleeding seemed to have stopped. Swapping to the other piece of fabric, she fashioned a bandage out of the strap that was left over and a cutting from the bottom of Shane's jeans jacket. It was difficult getting the bandage around him, as she didn't want him to start bleeding again. He helped as much as he could but finally fell unconscious. Nikki tied off the cloth and frowned at the dirty jacket part.

Shane slept the rest of the day. Nikki was able to nap for a bit. The discomfort from the bark of the tree she was slumped against eventually woke her. She watched the wind blow through the trees for a bit. It felt so peaceful, so different from the fear and violence of the past week—or two; she had truly lost track. She reached out to the knife Shane had given her. She looked it over. It was important—this much she knew. "This was your sister's," she whispered. Shane snorted in his sleep. She opened the long blade. It was attached to a black wooden hilt, with brass on the end. On the blade were two cranes beak to beak. "Kissing cranes, huh? Wonder if your boyfriend gave you this," she mumbled, trying to visualize what Shane's sister must have looked like.

"He did," Shane weakly answered. "How long have I been asleep?" He tried to sit up.

"Don't know; a couple of hours. How are you feeling?" She was next to him, helping him up.

"Like I've been shot, beaten, and stumbled through the woods." He laughed and then coughed. "How are you?"

"Oh, great except for the punch in the head, absolute terror, oh, and dragging your ass through the woods." She smiled back at him. She closed the blade and started to hand it back to him.

"No, you keep it. You need a weapon," he said, closing his eyes.

"What about you?" she asked, still holding the knife out.

He just picked up the gun that she forgot he had and waved it in the air.

"Oh, right." She brought her weapon back to her and looked at it again. Her boyfriend had given her a necklace once. "Interesting gift," she said before she could stop herself.

Shane did not open his eyes. "My sis liked knives, and Darren liked my sister. About the only thing, he did right." Shane moved an arm over his face and added, "Other than...end her."

"He killed his—your sister?" she gasped. Shane nodded. Nikki acted as if she couldn't see the tears that rolled down his face.

"When everyone started dying, I was over at a friend's house. His mother got really sick and then died, I guess, and got back up. I knew what was happening." Shane spoke from under his arm.

"I was out at dinner with my boyfriend," Nikki mumbled.

Shane nodded. "I think it was a Friday. Well, Tammy never would listen to me when I called her. I told her to stay home. She went over to Phil's house. I guess his family had turned, and she got bit." Shane paused. Nikki didn't push. She could feel the prickling behind her eyes. Shane took a deep breath. "He brought her back to the house. I got home…" Shane took another deep breath. Wincing, he gingerly touched his side. "I got home after she had turned and killed our dad." He swallowed. Nikki felt the first tear fall. "Phil grabbed the knife from her room and ran it through her skull." Shane lay silently for a moment. "I never liked that guy. We survived for a couple days before he got killed when we were trying to get food."

"I'm so sorry," Nikki whispered. Her tears fell for Shane's sister, for her family, and for Tim. She cried for all the loss.

"You were out on a date?" he asked.

"Yeah, Tim." She brushed the tears from her face. "Not sure what happened to him. Or my parents, my brother, my friends. I guess they are all dead now." She shrugged, her heart aching. "I ended up hiding in an attic above a store for…well, up until three days ago. Not sure how long I was there." She played with the hem of her jacket. She could see it was frayed in the dying light. "I saw a zombie that looked a lot like Tim when I was running out of town. Didn't stop to see if it was him." The silence dragged on.

"Rest. We'll try to get to my uncle's tomorrow," he said.

"You need to rest," she countered. He didn't seem to hear her.

"We need food and water. That isn't going to happen here," he stated. She nodded even though Shane still had his face covered. When sleep came, it was a chaotic mess. Zombie Shane was eating Tim's arm while a young girl who looked like Shane nailed leathered hands to a roof.

Some Are Here and Some Are Gone

Creepy and Criey had gone, and Mary did not miss them. Chris spent most of his time hanging around Hayley. Gwen just smirked every time she saw this. Mary just found it annoying. Hayley was far too old for her brother. Then petty thoughts like that were drowned out by the moans of the dead from the floor below.

The other apartments around them had been opened up and picked clean. At first, Mary and Chris were going to move into one, but their first night was so terrifying that they returned to the group. It got easier after the other two had left. Mary still wished she had a place of her own.

"How much longer do you think we can stay here?" Mary whispered to Chris as they took stock of the food. They were beginning to get down to beans and stale cereal.

"We're going to have to do a grocery run soon, that's for sure," Hayley interrupted.

"No one asked you," Mary muttered, earning her a swipe from Chris.

"They may not have. But nonetheless, we need to find food." Hayley smiled at a red-faced Mary. "There are apartments below us that we know have zombies." She looked up. "There are also apartments above us that…we have no idea what is up there."

"I don't know. Mary and I heard footsteps from up there," Chris offered, earning him a glare from Mary. She had heard them, and that was part of the reason they returned to the group, but she didn't want them to know that.

"Well, known or unknown?" Gwen had joined the conversation. "We'll have to deal with both eventually."

"Well, I vote for the upstairs. We know what is below us," Hayley offered. Arms crossed, she looked up at the ceiling. "Besides, the thumping I heard seemed quite light."

"That makes it easier? Better? What if its…What if there are…" Mary stuttered. She had seen them at the rescue center. They were horrific—little hands covered in blood; the cold, dead eyes; little teeth that could do so much damage. "You don't understand, there might be children…dead children," Mary finished in a whisper. The silence in the room told her this was something they had not thought of.

The four of them were at the foot of the stairs, looking up. A motley arrangement of weapons was in their hands: Gwen held a brass lamp base, Chris had a large carving knife, and Hayley had her gun and a baseball bat. Mary held tight to a bread knife. Chris laughed at her choice at first. She explained the logic.

"If we run into the living, the serrated edge will do a ton of damage. Remember when I cut my hand up washing the one at home?" Chris cringed at the memory. "Plus it is long. I can jab it"—she thrust it out in front of her at eye level—"into an eye socket, and down it goes." She nodded as if that explained it all.

"Good strategy," Hayley affirmed, giving Mary's shoulder a pat. Mary shrugged it off but was proud of the compliment, and it annoyed Chris.

Now, looking up into the dim stairwell, the weapon seemed laughable as did her bravado. If something came out of the dark at her, she was sure she'd just run. Together they were climbing the stairs slowly, one by one.

"Why are we doing this?" Mary hissed.

"So we don't starve to death," Chris grumbled back.

"So we will be more filling when the dead eat us?" she shot back.

"Shhhh!" Gwen hushed. Mary felt as if she was back with her mother for a second. The thought tugged at her heart. They were at the top of the stairs, looking down a hall that was an exact duplicate of the one they just left. A door halfway down thudded shut. They froze in their tracks; the silence was deafening.

"They don't close doors; they come after us," Hayley whispered.

"Unless they get stuck behind the door. I saw one that did that," Mary replied, quickly releasing Hayley's sleeve. She wasn't sure when she had grabbed it. No one seemed to notice.

Gwen's hand pushed down the gun Hayley was holding. She moved to the first door and pointed to her eyes and then to Hayley, and then to the door that shut. Chris was ushered to Gwen's side while Mary was signaled to watch the stairs. Mary glanced over her shoulder to watch in wonder as Gwen jumped up a little while pushing down on the apartment's doorknob. The door sprang open, and Chris and Gwen jumped back. Nothing happened. The pair disappeared into the room. Mary slowly retreated until she was near Hayley and she could glance into the apartment. Some knocked-over furniture and scattered clothing were all she could see.

There was a sudden pressure against her back. Mary jumped and then realized it was Hayley standing back to back with her. Mary heard a soft whisper. "I'm scared shitless. How are you holding up?"

"No problem," Mary lied. She thought for a second and added, "No, I am fucking terrified." She exhaled.

"Oh, thank God, I thought it was just me." Hayley sighed. They stood back to back, shaking slightly, until both let out a nervous laugh. Still about to burst from fear, Mary let herself relax a little. She decided to trust and maybe even like Hayley.

Long Road

When the morning came, it was apparent Shane was too weak to move. Even though she didn't want to leave the safety of their nest or her weak companion, Nikki descended the ladder. Her stomach told her she really had no choice. They had not eaten since the previous morning. She knew Shane needed her to find something to eat.

Twenty minutes in, Nikki knew she was way out of her element. "What the hell am I doing?" she demanded of the sky. "I should be in Civics right now, not searching the woods in the fall looking for nuts and berries." She kicked at the leaves and pine needles. Her foot slipped; she moved to steady herself, lost her balance, and hit the ground. Anger flared for a second. She wanted to scream until she saw the mushrooms. Collecting as many as she could, Nikki returned. Along the way, she had found a few berries as well. "No nuts, but I got some nonpoisonous mushrooms and berries. I hope."

Shane was able to lift himself up on one elbow to inspect her find. "Not bad." He smiled. "None of this will kill us."

"Unlike everything else in the world." Nikki frowned. After splitting the meager items, with her secretly giving more to Shane, they ate in silence. After their meal, Nikki felt even hungrier, if anything. By midafternoon Nikki was helping Shane replace the soaked bandage.

"What is this?" he asked, placing a torn piece of his T-shirt over the hole.

"You mean what was it?" Nikki replied with a grimace as she threw the blood-soaked former bra cup over the edge. "It

was a bra. I grabbed it in this shop on my way out of town."
She looked at the smirk on his face. "What? It was clean.
You're just lucky I had it," she grumbled, scratching absently
at her side where she could envision her current garment was
filthy against her skin.

"Well, thanks. I appreciate your sacrifice." Shane laughed
and immediately regretted it. He moaned and lay back down.
"Damn it, I shouldn't have let you toss that over. Might bring
them here."

"Great time to think of that." She frowned. She clambered
down the ladder. It took her several minutes to find the soiled
bandages. She took them far away, returning with more
mushrooms and berries. The berries were sour, and the
mushrooms were disgusting. They had no water; Shane had
warned her not to drink from anything she found in the woods.
On her return, she found Shane was asleep. His shallow
breathing made her nervous. As the day wore on, the weather
turned colder.

*You've seen enough movies to know we need to share body
heat*, she told herself. Then the little voice in the back of her
head spoke the fear she was trying to avoid. *If he dies, you'll be
that much closer.* Then the third voice she never wanted to hear
spoke up. *Yeah, and if I die, then at least this will all be over.*
She shivered with cold and fear. "Looks like it's two against
one," she muttered. She moved next to him, trying to decide
the best course. She ended up lying against his back. It was
only slightly warmer.

Between the shivering and the sound of the undead in the
forest, Nikki slept very little. She was glad she had taken the
bandage away. The morning sun found Shane pale but moving

better. "God, if I look half as bad as you…" he began but was silenced by her giving him the finger. "Sorry." He laughed, flinching as he did. "I think we need to find a new place to stay." He was in a seated position.

"You think you can make it down the ladder, you big sissy?" she asked as he groaned.

"I won't be running any races, but I think we can get moving, yeah." He had already slowly made his way to the ladder.

"Should I go first, just in case?" she asked.

He scoffed. "In case what? You gonna catch me?"

"No, in case you fall, I can get a better view as you bounce," she shot back at him.

"Please don't make me laugh!" He laughed anyway, holding his side. Nikki made it down and waited as he descended the ladder slowly and joined her at the bottom. Nikki was looking around and then at him, expectantly.

"So which way?"

Getting his bearings, he pointed to the north and began to limp off. She followed close behind, helping him every so often over logs. After about an hour, they reached an embankment. Shane struggled to make it up, Nikki helping as much as she could. "Remind me not to like you," she grunted, pulling him the last couple of feet.

"Noted," he gasped. Catching his breath, he sighed in relief at finding they were on a road. He looked to his left, then right, and then left again.

"I don't think anyone is coming," Nikki noted.

"Huh?"

"It is safe to cross." She pointed to the other side.

"No, I think we can follow this, but which way?" he muttered. After several moments he made up his mind. He turned right. Nikki followed. They made better time on the flat surface. Nikki liked the feeling of safety of walking in the middle of the road. She knew it was only slightly safer, but being out of the woods made her a little happier.

Slowly they crested a hill. What they saw did not cause them to increase their pace. Up ahead they saw a truck half off the road. Pulling their few weapons, they approached cautiously. The truck was smashed into a tree. There were a couple of gallon jugs lying on the road. Abandoning caution, Nikki rushed to them. She quickly opened one. The smell was overwhelming as she opened one. "Gas—they are all gas," she whimpered.

Shane understood her disappointment. His own mouth felt like a desert. Moving past her, he began to check the cab of the truck. "Nik, hey," he called her over.

"Nikki," she grumbled as she joined him at the cab. Smiling, he handed her a bottle of water and showed her a can of chili. Her smile matched his. She took a long draft of the water and then handed him the bottle. He took it and finished it. "Hey!" she shouted. "We should have rationed that!"

Smiling, he reached into the truck. He turned back to face her with two more bottles of water and another knife. Cracking open the chili with their new knife, he handed her the can. It was the most delicious thing Nikki could ever remember tasting. They sat on the tailgate of the truck, eating the chili and drinking the warm water. A little color had returned to Shane's face.

After several minutes of sitting in silence, he looked over at her. She nodded. Returning to the cab of the truck, they took the last of the water, each stuffing a bottle of water in their jackets, and continued down the road. About a mile from the truck, they came across another car. This one was sitting in the middle of the road. Shane held out an arm, stopping Nikki. There was something about this that bothered him. Nikki placed a hand on his arm. "Keep an eye out," she whispered.

Cautiously she approached the vehicle. There was a bloodstain on the side of the car. On the road, her eyes followed a long blood smear leading away from the door into the woods. Opening the door she covered her mouth, feeling the chili jump into her throat. The inside had blood covering the seats and dash. Bloody handprints on the windows told of a struggle. Something caught her attention. She looked into the back seat. She could see the child's car seat. Jumping away from the car, she yelled. Shane rushed to her side.

"No, no, no, *no!*" she shouted.

"Shhhh," Shane cautioned while looking inside. In the car seat was an infant. Its skin was already starting to peel away from the skull. It reached out to Shane and gurgled, oozing black goo over blackened lips. Nikki turned away when Shane opened the door. The gurgling of the zombie became audible as he did. She wanted to run away, but then it was silent. Nikki sank to her knees in the middle of the deserted road and cried, cried as she had not done since she was a little girl. Getting a hold of her tears, panic now threatened to overtake her as she heard something get thrown in the woods. She wanted to run.

She wanted to be home. She wanted to curl up in a ball and never move again. There were some sounds like a car trying to start, but she ignored them. After several minutes she felt hands gently pull her to her feet.

"The car appears to be OK...except..." he spoke calmly, soothingly.

"Wa-wa-what?" she sniffled.

He looked down sheepishly. "I think...I think it is just out of gas."

The implication of his statement took a moment to sink in. "Oh God, you mean we have to walk all the way back to the truck?" she sobbed.

"Yeah. Come on." He wrapped an arm around her, and they began the long walk back. "By the way, you have to carry the gas; I'm injured," he said.

She tried to smile. "You *will* be injured," she said.

The walk back was a blur to Nikki. She was trying to block what she had seen from her mind. For his part, Shane kept talking. He told her about an old car he wanted to buy. He told stories of sneaking out at night with his friends. Some of his tales, Nikki was pretty sure, were made up just to entertain her. Finally, they reached the truck and gathered a couple of the containers of gas together.

"We'll leave most of them here—just take two gallons and then come back for the rest," Shane said while holding his side. Blood had seeped through the bandage again. Nikki checked the truck and found a first-aid kit they had overlooked the first time.

"Great, the aspirin will take care of this." Shane grimaced at his side.

She spared him one look before unpacking a bandage. It took a few minutes to change out the bloody wrapping. Shane was pale again. It took him a long time to ease off the tailgate. Nikki grabbed two of the gallon jugs and waited for Shane to get to his feet. He was still leaning heavily on the truck. He smiled at her as if to say he was fine. She wasn't fooled. The shadows were getting longer, and she was anxious to get back to the other car before dark.

The trip back was slow. The jugs seemed to gain weight with every step, and Shane seemed to get slower. Even in the fading light, she could see he was very pale. He spoke very little. She kept having to shake a thought from her mind—the thought that he might not last much longer. So it was her turn to keep up the steady stream of stories. Nothing as interesting as his, she thought, but he did perk up a little when she mentioned wanting a motorcycle.

The trees began to press in on them as the sky changed from blue to gray. It would soon be black out, with no light except the stars and moon. The power was out in the cities, so the night had regained its darkness. It was this darkness that urged Nikki forward, burdened as she was. It seemed to take twice as long to get back to the car as it took to get to the truck. The feelings of fear grew with each step. She wanted, needed, to be in that car. It was too open here, too dark. Finally, they were back. Tears of relief ran down her face. Stumbling the last few feet, Shane slumped against the side of the car, his breathing labored.

"Get in; I'll fill the tank." Her voice was breaking with stress. Darkness was overtaking them quickly. As it did, the noises from the woods amplified. Shane opened the passenger-side door and called her over. When Nikki reached his side, he looked terrible in the yellow interior light.

He handed her a funnel. "You'll need this to get the gas in the tank." Then he pressed the gun into her hand. "You may need this…for me."

Panic threatened to overtake her. Her hands shook as she pushed the gun back to him. Swallowing her fear, she looked him in the eye. "Well, you can't die. I…I don't know where I am going, and…"—she cast around for a reason—"and I only have a learner's permit, so I have to have a licensed driver with me."

Coughing, Shane laughed. "Well, in that case, I guess I have to be OK."

"Damn right; now, get in the car." She eased him into the seat. He laughed weakly as she snapped the seatbelt on. She hurried to the back of the car and worked the funnel into the tank. She shook badly, spilling gas over the pavement as she tried to fill it. Her head whipped this way and that way with every sound. The second jug empty, she dropped it and hurried to the door. She tried the handle and it was locked. "Why the hell did we lock this?" She gasped.

A twig snapped to her left. A shuffling sound from a shadow ahead. She began to panic again; she rattled the handle; the door gave, and she stumbled back. Shane had barely slumped back into his seat out of her way as she jumped in. Slamming the door, she relocked it. Gasping, she glanced at Shane. His eyes were barely slits.

Trying to get her breathing under control, she turned the key. The engine whirred but did not turn over. She pumped the gas and tried again. "Wrrr-wrrr-wrrr." Something hit the back of the car. Nikki's eyes flicked up to the rearview mirror. The corpse's face pressed against the glass of the back window. "Oh, Christ!" She fumbled for the key again.

"Wrr-wrr-wrr," said the car.

"Unnnnggghhhh," responded the woods.

"Oh shit, oh shit, oh shit!" she cried while bouncing in her seat, urging the car to start.

"Wrr-wrr-wrr-wrrrrrroar!" The engine burst into life. Hands hit her window, and she screamed. A zombie began to pound on the hood. She looked out Shane's window and saw bloody hands pressed against it.

"Get us out of here!" Shane yelled while grabbing her by the shoulders and shaking her. His eyes were huge. Nikki turned back to the wheel and slammed the accelerator to the floor. Nothing happened.

"Put it in gear, girl!" Shane screamed.

"Don't yell at me!" she screamed back. As she threw the car into drive, the engine caught, and the tires squealed. The face in the back and the hands on the windows were gone. But the zombie in front clung to the hood. Nikki slammed on the brakes. The zombie slid off with a thud. She pulled the headlights on and screamed, throwing herself against the seat. The road was full of zombies with more pouring out of the woods by the second.

"Go, go, go!" Shane hissed. His color was white, but there was life in his eyes. He was still with her, for the moment.

Teeth gritting, she turned the wheel, threw it back in drive, and smashed the accelerator. They slammed into two zombies and thumped over a third. Pulling the wheel over, she aimed for another zombie. She reached the side of the road, slammed on the brakes, and threw it in reverse. The transmission clicked a few times and then caught as she slammed down the accelerator.

"Stop, stop!" Shane yelled as she almost went into a ditch.

"I told you to stop yelling at me!" she growled. Turning the wheel and putting the car back in drive, she barreled through the undead mass.

"Why does—" thump of a zombie against the hood, "everyone—" smack of a ghoul off the side-view mirror, "always—" she swung the wheel to run down another zombie, "yell when I drive?" She turned to glare at Shane.

He had one hand on the dash and the other on the ceiling of the car, bracing himself. "Because your driving is scarier than the dead," he said, wide-eyed.

"Whatever," she grumbled and slammed through a small group, sending them flailing like bowling pins. The road was finally clear.

No Longer a Certainty

Alistair sat watching Washington burn. A long line of military vehicles passed by the camera, the same as they had seen in Philadelphia and New York. Rebecca had not said a word in a while. As the helicopter picture showed the capitol building in flames, Alistair noticed the look on her face.

"What in the world is funny?" Alistair demanded of his wife.

"It's just..." she seemed to struggle. "It's just there is nothing left for certain."

"There never was anything. Why do you think we built this place?"

"No, no," she replied. "You remember the old saying. Nothing is certain except for death and taxes..." She watched as it dawned on him. "That's right, neither is certain anymore."

Two More to Go

Gwen and Hayley whispered in the corner of the room. Mary sat alone, pretending to read a worn-out copy of an H. P. Lovecraft collection. Chris sat with the two kids they had found hiding in an apartment on the floor above. They had brought them and all the food they could back down. One of the kids was called Squeaker by Chris because that was all he did. The little girl was named Lucinda. They thought the two were siblings until Lucinda corrected them. "He is a nice boy, quiet, but I don't know his name," she had explained.

Squeaker would point at something and squeak. He would answer questions with a head nod or shake. Gwen theorized why this was. "I would bet his parents told him to keep quiet. When faced with the horrors, he couldn't." She sighed. "I bet he thinks he is responsible for their deaths." Mary thought this was stupid. She spent a lot of time with the boy but never tried to get him to speak like the others. She would just talk to him. It felt good talking about things with someone who didn't ask questions, interrupt, or try to help. Chris agreed with Hayley that Mary shouldn't be burdening the kid with her problems.

"I'm not telling him anything he doesn't know," Mary protested one night. "He has seen some shit, I can guarantee that. Instead of just listening to him squeak, I think the more we share with him, the more he will open up."

"Are you kidding me right now?" Chris demanded. "All that stuff you went through at the rescue center—that is stuff no kid needs to hear. Hell, I don't want to hear it."

"Well, I'm so sorry what I went through annoys you." Mary's voice began to rise. "At least someone here listens."

"What, a kid who doesn't talk back and can't tell you to shut up?" Chris's voice rose to meet hers. "Oh, and because I didn't see anything? I didn't see Dad eating Denise from next door! I didn't see Mom coming out of the kitchen with her guts hanging out! I didn't watch parts of Denise fall out of Dad's mouth as she got up and the three of them started to come after me!"

"You said the house burned," Mary said softly.

"It did. Who do you think set the fire?" Chris was crying now.

"Why didn't you tell me?"

"How could I? I had just picked you up from that bloodbath. What did you want me to say?" Chris swiped at his eyes. "Hey, Mary, I know you've been through some shit, but I just burned up our dead zombie parents and the nice lady who used to babysit us." His back was turned to her. Mary's hand hovered over his shoulder. She tried to touch him, but he pulled away. Squeaker had appeared in the doorway. He walked past Mary to crouch in front of Chris.

In a voice cracking and barely audible, the boy spoke. "Not your fault." The words sounded painful to him. He rubbed his throat. "Not my fault." He reached out to hug Chris. He looked over Chris's shoulder at Mary and Hayley. "Dead people's fault."

On the Last Leg

The last zombie had banged off the car several minutes before. With the road cleared out in front of them, Nikki let up on the accelerator. Her legs shook, and her hands ached. She flexed the fingers of each hand, trying to get the feeling back. She checked the rearview mirror and could not see any of the undead. Shane relaxed into his seat, breathing heavily and holding his side.

"You doing OK?" she ventured.

He just nodded. The adrenaline was fading, and so was he. He was shivering even as the heater began to work. Distracted as she was with the mirror and her passenger, Nikki was surprised at how quickly they returned to the fuel. Coming up on the truck, she slowed and turned around to head back in the right direction. Stopping as close as she could to the fuel they had collected, she left the car running.

"You just relax, OK? We'll be cruising down the road to your uncle's in no time." Nikki jumped out, scrambling for the jugs. Cursing, she dropped one of the plastic jugs and returned to the car to get the funnel. "Just hold on, OK? Be done in a second." Shane gave a weak thumbs-up. Gas splashed again as she poured another two gallons into the tank. She reached for a third, hesitated, and put it in the back of the car. She looked around, grabbed all the jugs she could, and loaded them, five gallons in all, into the back. Feeling it was loaded enough, she began to pour the last gallon into the tank. Over the glug-glug of the emptying plastic, she heard them approaching on the road. The low moaning and the scraping shuffling met her ears even from a distance.

"Screw this!" she breathed as the headlights began to illuminate the mass of walking undead. There was some gas left, but she wasn't wasting any more time. The jug flew from her hand, landing with an empty clatter on the road. She was back in the driver's seat before the jug came to rest.

"I know what you are going to say, so I don't know why I am asking but," taking a deep breath, she pressed on, "but are you sure this is the way do we need to go?"

Shane cracked an eye and sighed, pointing in the direction of the oncoming dead.

"Knew it." She grimaced as she locked the door, buckled her seat belt, and put the car in drive. Picking up speed she rammed into the wall of corpses.

Haven

The sun began its slow ascent into the sky. Alistair switched from the night-vision scope to his regular binoculars. He was always an early riser, but he rarely was up before the sun. Something was coming; he could feel it. Retreating from the open air of the tower to the observation room below, he checked the bank of monitors showing the various fence lines and gates. Nothing appeared out of the ordinary.

When Alistair bought this place from the government, there was only one perimeter fence. Now there were four of them. One ran the length of the road, ten feet high, topped with razor wire. A half mile from there was the second fence. This was also ten feet high, but it had a wire at the bottom and top. A mile after that was the third fence. This was fifteen feet high with metal spikes every few feet, sticking out at an angle. It looked as if something used to stop charging cavalry. The final line of defense was four twenty-foot-tall walls, three feet thick with iron spikes and razor wire along the top. A trench ran the length of it. It would cause an attacker to be exposed and have to climb out into gunfire. That was what it was designed for. The building inside the wall had been a missile silo. The grand house above the ten-foot-thick door was formidable enough before one even got into the bunker. It had steel metal shutters, reinforced walls, thick doors, and places to shoot from. It had two towers from which a sniper could take out targets in relative safety. The building could withstand several hits from RPGs.

Checking the cameras, Alistair noted there were now three of the creatures wandering around the front fence near the front gate. From the grainy video, he couldn't tell for sure but thought one of them could have been the foreman who helped build the house. Shaking the thought, he flipped through about half of the twenty or so cameras. He let the images flash by not really taking them in until movement caught his eye. He flipped back to the image in question, thinking it would be a deer. Alistair's feet, which had been up on the console, hit the floor. His full attention was now on the monitor. Between the second and third fences, shuffling through the dry leaves and brush was one of the undead.

"How in the hell did you get in there?" he asked the zombie, tapping on the monitor as he did. It didn't seem to be doing any harm or seem to have any destination. It just wandered aimlessly through the brush. Carefully he rechecked all the gates leading to the compound. They were all closed. "You didn't climb over the fence," he muttered, clicking through several more images.

Alistair spent the next half hour systematically surveying the area from the walls of the compound to the first of the fences. The smell of coffee met his nostrils, and he turned to smile at his wife.

"You're up early, thanks," he said while taking the cup from her.

"You're one to talk. What's up?" Rebecca asked, taking a seat next to him. She began to check motion sensors, noting one was flashing.

"Not sure," he said, shrugging, "just a weird feeling."

"Did you see a sensor was tripped?" she asked.

"Yeah, one got in. Can't seem to figure out how, though."

"So how's our new friend liking the accommodations?"

Alistair laughed. "Just wandering around." He switched a monitor over to the camera that showed the lost zombie as it fell over a log. Alistair sipped his coffee, watching the ghoul struggle to its feet. "Wonder what he did before?" Alistair wondered aloud.

Rebecca poked him in the shoulder and pointed to the monitor that featured the gate to the driveway off the main road. "We might have some trouble."

"What do you want?" Alistair asked the car that was sitting very close to the gate. "Damn it," he grumbled, expecting the car to ram through the wire fence. The gate was held closed with a thick chain and combination lock. He was going for intimidating without being too obvious. He didn't want nosy people investigating. His fist clenched as he prepared to watch his first line of defense fall.

Instead, the drivers-side door opened, and a young woman ran out to the lock. She turned back, running to the passenger window. She poked her head in. She was out a half jump back to the fence and then returned to the window. Alistair squinted at the small black-and-white picture. The zombies were also watching the progress. They were moving toward the car.

"Are they trying to figure out the combination?" Rebecca asked over his shoulder.

"Looks like they did!" Alistair found himself on his feet. His voice was an octave higher in surprise. Rebecca had a hold of his arm as he stood up straight. He never took his eye off the screen. The girl ran back to the car and pulled through the gate. "What the hell?" Alistair shouted. Stunned, he looked at his wife, who stared back in shock. The intruder had jumped back out of the car, closed the gate, and appeared to relock it.

"Just in time, too," Rebecca commented as three zombies shuffled up fast to the closed gate. The girl backed away and appeared to…"Did she just give them the finger?" Rebecca laughed.

"Is that one of your family? Your niece?" Alistair asked.

Rebecca studied the monitor as the car sped to the next gate. The girl jumped out again. "No, the hair is too dark. She has the key, though." The second gate swung open, and the car was through. Again the gate was closed and relocked. "I don't recognize her. I like her, though. Are you sure that isn't Tammy?"

"No, that isn't her. Too tall. She might be the one telling the driver the combos," Alistair commented. "It has to be someone who knows about us. Or someone told them about us. Did you check on your sister today?"

"Yeah, Krissy was running all over, chasing the cat. Oh shit." Rebecca was looking at another monitor. Alistair threw her a questioning look. "Well, whoever they are, they have a problem. The next gate is another combination lock, and our new friend seems to know they are here." Rebecca pointed to the zombie that was in the fence line. He had become very attentive and then started to move with purpose toward the driveway and the gate.

"They better hurry," Alistair urged as the car skidded to a halt, and the girl was out again. She turned to the car and gestured frantically. She worked the lock and then yelled back to the car. A head leaned out the window, resting on the frame.

"Shane!" Alistair yelled. "It's our nephew." He was jumping up and down. "Come on, girl, hurry!" The lock was off, and she was driving through. "I can't see Tam." He tried to look around Shane through the monitor.

"Leave it, just leave it," Rebecca whispered as the car stopped. Nikki jumped out to close the gate. She could smell the zombie, hear its moan, but couldn't see it. She got the gate closed.

Just as she was reattaching the lock—"Look out! Look out!" Shane started yelling out the window. He was trying to point. Nikki looked around frantically. She saw it moving up to her quickly. Dropping the chain, Nikki ran to the passenger side of the car. Her feet slipped in the gravel. She caught herself, holding a sprinter's stance.

"Get in, get in!" the couple urged the images on the monitor. Nikki just ran to the front of the car. The zombie was confused as to which way to go. She was running past it. It reached out but missed. She was back to the passenger side, waving her arms.

"She's baiting it," Alistair breathed. The zombie moved to the passenger side, and Nikki ran to the driver's door and jumped in. The zombie clawed at the window as the car sped off. Alistair fell back into his chair, covering his eyes with his arm. Rebecca rubbed his shoulders.

"Brave girl," she told her husband. She was watching the dust rise from the speeding vehicle. They were at the last gate before the main gate at the wall. Again they opened and relocked the gate. "Alistair! Go let them in," his wife reminded him with a smack to the arm.

Standing up with a start, Alistair leaned in and kissed his wife. He bounded down the stairs from the tower to the ledge around the wall. He quickly made his way along the walkway along the top of the wall behind the thick cover to the front gate. He arrived at the same moment the car skidded to a halt.

Nikki stuck her head out of the window and shouted, "Please let us in! I'm with Shane, and he is hurt." Her face was tense and sweat-soaked.

The excitement left Alistair, immediately replaced by dread. "Was he bitten?" His hand quickly found the handgun he kept at his side. "He can't—neither of you can come in if you're bitten."

"What? No, he was shot! Please let us in," Nikki called.

Alistair hesitated. His hand hovered over the button. "Open the damn gate!" she yelled. Alistair pushed the button to open the gate. The car was through and the gate began to reclose. Its heavy steel squealed in the track. Rebecca was running from the house to the car as Alistair made his way to a ladder. He watched the driver fly to the passenger door. Finally, he was at the bottom, on the ground, across the courtyard. When he reached the car, both women were helping Shane out.

"Hey, Uncle," Shane weakly greeted him.

Uncomfortable

"Hey, Dad, do you smell that?" Kyle glanced over at his father. Ray frowned as he noticed Kyle's hair was still a mess from sleeping. Ray, who had woken early that day, lowered his book and sniffed at the air.

"OK, that isn't good," he noted, rising from his chair. Krissy, still in her pajamas, and Jennifer met them in the hall.

"You smell that, right?" Jennifer asked.

"It's OK. I'm sure it is coming from outside," Ray assured his family even as he and Kyle were checking the guns and heading to the door.

"I smell barbecue." Krissy sniffed deeply. "Are we having steaks? For breakfast?"

"Um…no, that would be, um…" Ray faltered.

"I think it might be coming from some other house," Kyle lied. "People we haven't met."

"What people?" she demanded. "People like us? Not dead?"

Kyle glanced at his father, who shrugged back. Neither knew how to explain. Jennifer directed her daughter over to the screen. "Let's see what Uncle Alistair can see, huh, honey?" Ray nodded his thanks. He headed out the door toward the ladder leading up to the catwalk around the wall. The smell was oppressive out here. Smoke lingered in the courtyard.

"Wherever it is, it's close," Kyle surmised as he followed his father up the ladder.

"Not so close as it is widespread," Ray replied, looking out toward the town. The sky was deep red and orange. Smoke billowed across the horizon. "Looks like downtown is burning."

Kyle looked around at the other houses close by. "Looks like we should be OK. Lots of distance between places here."

"God, that smell." Ray covered his nose and face with his hand. "How many of those things you think are burning up?"

"Daddy, Mommy says she can't get Uncle Alistair on the phone. What things are burning?" Krissy asked. Ray jumped and stuttered. The arrival of his daughter had gone completely unnoticed.

"Dad was just talking about the buildings downtown," Kyle attempted to cover.

"Oh, Daddy meant the zombies were burning. It's gross, but it doesn't smell so bad." Krissy shrugged before climbing back down the ladder and skipping across the courtyard, disappearing through the door. Ray and Kyle could do nothing but stare in stunned silence.

"That was disturbing," Kyle admitted. His father nodded vigorously.

Bunker

Alistair grabbed Shane's shoulders, taking over for an exhausted, struggling Nikki, while Rebecca had his feet. Nikki held onto Shane's hand as he was rushed through the front door. The lights blinded her, as did the shine on the floor and walls. Glancing back, she was shocked at the trail of muddy footprints and blood. Alistair yelled something at her, kicking at a closed door.

"I'll be right back," she told Shane. He did not respond. Quickly she threw open the door behind Alistair. They were in a bedroom. She flipped on the light. The room was clean and comfortable. Against the wall was a large bed, on which Alistair and Rebecca laid Shane. Rebecca asked her husband for several things that Nikki didn't really hear. Shane was ghostly pale by now. Alistair pushed past her. She heard his feet thunder down the hall. Seconds later he was back, with a medical bag in hand.

Nikki couldn't see what was going on, but it didn't appear Shane was responding to any questions. "I got you here," Nikki whispered. Rebecca was using a respirator on him. "I got you here, so *you damn well better be OK!*" she shouted. She tried to push past the couple to get at Shane. This wasn't funny. He needed to get up and say something to her.

Rebecca gave Alistair a look. He took a violently protesting Nikki by the shoulders and steered her out of the room. She fought him all the way out; he could barely control her flailing. "Shhhh, shhhh," he tried to reassure her. "My wife is a trained doctor; we'll do everything we can for him."

"He can't die. You hear me? He can't—he's my only friend. I need him to be OK," Nikki stormed. "He can't become one of them." She threw off his grip but did not attempt to reenter the room. "You will save him if you know what's good for you," she threatened, even though Alistair stood a good foot and a half taller and was built like a linebacker. "He will not become one!" she mumbled.

Alistair held her by the shoulders again, this time loosely. He looked her straight in the eye. "No matter what...he won't."

Nikki returned the stare. Suddenly she was exhausted. Her legs wobbled and shook. Her eyes rolled as she no longer was able to stand. Alistair quickly grabbed her arms as she began to sink. Holding her upright, he noted the hopelessness in her eyes. Tears streamed down her face.

"Rebecca will take care of him; he'll be fine. Why don't you get cleaned up? I'll bring you some clean clothes, and you can get a shower," he offered, holding her up. She fought to stand on her own.

Nikki stared at him; how could she possibly get a shower when Shane was lying there so close to death? She tried to push him out of the way but found limp noodles where her arms should have been. She was so tired.

Alistair steered her down the hall to another room. It had a large bed and a bathroom. Alistair helped her to a chair by a desk. She could see into the bathroom. It contained a huge shower in a beautifully tiled room. Looking back at the room, she was reminded of a luxury hotel she had seen an ad for. Alistair stepped out for a moment and then returned with a pile of folded clothes.

"These should fit. Take your time with the shower," he said, collecting towels and other toiletries. "I just checked with Rebecca. Shane is going to be OK. Rebecca is quite a good doctor. He will likely be sleeping, but you can visit him when you're done." The thought of a visit allowed her to breathe again. Letting out something between a laugh and a sob, she nodded at him. "We'll get you something to eat, and then you can tell me how you got here." He closed the door, leaving Nikki in a clean, beautiful room. She stood up; halfway to the door, she looked around again.

It was unreal. For days she had been cold, starving, and hunted. Now she was in a beautiful room inside a fortress. She was safe—she hoped—but couldn't relax. The only person she knew in the whole world was hurt, and she had no idea if he was actually OK or if this Alistair just said that to calm her down. Doubt crept in; she didn't know these people. She remembered the crazy man at the cabin, and suddenly the urge to run came over her.

Taking a few calming breaths, she reminded herself aloud, "I trust Shane. These are family members of his. I can trust them." Her arms encircled herself protectively. She started to sit down on the bed but stopped, looking down at her filthy, torn, bloody clothes. It didn't seem right to sit on the clean, white bedding. She wandered around the room for a few moments before sinking to the floor. She had so far been able to avoid looking in the mirror, not wanting to see just how horrid she looked.

She sat on the floor, looking at the older sculpted carpet with patterns running through the pile. She didn't know how long she sat there, studying the patterns in the thick rug, but her legs were cramped and falling asleep. She jumped at the knock on the door. Rebecca looked in. "Shane is doing OK. He lost a lot of blood, and the wound looks infected, but I think we got to it in time. He is resting now." Nikki had backed to the wall when the door opened. "It is OK; you're safe here." Rebecca smiled at Nikki.

Nikki held onto her confusion. Who was this woman? It took a moment to sink in. Shane was going to be OK. She was in some kind of a bunker; she was safe. Shane was going to be OK. Nikki slowly returned the smile. "Thank you," she croaked, not having spoken for a long time.

"Get cleaned up, and we'll get you something to eat," Rebecca urged. She then left Nikki alone again. The weight began to lift, and Nikki noticed how hungry she was and how truly disgusting she felt. Getting up, she caught sight of herself in the mirror. Her clothes were a camouflage of mud, stains, and filth. Her hair was matted. It contained twigs, mud, and caked blood. Everywhere she looked she saw blood—Shane's, hers, other things. Her face was obscured by dirt and even more blood. Tenderly she reached up to touch the puckered wound on her forehead. Her hand flew back as she squeaked. A single tear cleared a path down her cheek. For the first time, she noticed the smell coming off her.

Nikki let the water run over her head and down her back. It seemed like years since she had a shower. She watched the dirt and blood swirl and then disappear down the drain. She didn't want to waste water, but Alistair said there was plenty and to take her time, so she did. The warm water, the sound of normalcy, and the isolation all caused her to never want to leave the large, glass-enclosed shower with its waterfall shower head and body jets. *This is better than any hotel we ever stayed in*, she thought, closing her eyes. Laying her head on her arm, she leaned against the shower wall. This was something she definitely missed. She washed her hair twice and enjoyed the feel of the soap on her skin. Her hunger was the only thing that forced her to leave the warmth of the water.

Wrapped in a fluffy towel, she returned to the room. On the bed, folded neatly, was a T-shirt and sweatpants. "Oh God, is there anything more wonderful than clean clothes?" she moaned as she pulled on the garments. Clean for the first time in days, she took a moment to lie on the bed. The softness enveloped her. "I never appreciated how awesome a bed is," she mumbled into the fresh pillow. Her stomach grumbled while memories of outside rushed in. Immediately Nikki was on her feet and at the door.

Her hand rested on the knob, shaking. Her mind kept telling her it was OK, but then a thought would jump in. She would open this door and be back in the woods. Shane would have died and come back. Slowly she turned the knob. Inhaling deeply, she pushed the door slowly. The damp, musty leaves blew across her bare feet. Gaping-mouthed, Shane lunged at her. Her screams filled the room.

Nikki rolled off the bed, hitting the floor hard. Scrambling under the bed, she waited; nothing could be heard except the rapid in and out of her breathing. She had fallen asleep—how had that happened? Easing back out into the room, she stood up slowly. She was painfully aware that she was unarmed. That had to change. She was back at the door. Steeling herself, she swung the door open.

Stepping into the soft light of the hall, Nikki listened for trouble. Her footfalls echoed as she retraced her steps down the hall to the room where they had taken Shane. Digging deep, she readied for the worst. Her hand held firmly on the knob, yet refused to turn it. The silence was broken like a gunshot in her ears. Nikki flew to the far wall, backing away.

"How long you gonna stand there? It's OK, you can go in," Rebecca said, frowning. "Oh sorry, didn't mean to spook you." Rebecca took a step forward but held as Nikki retreated. "Saw some shit out there, did you?" Nikki nodded. "I'm not going to hurt you. I promise you are safe here."

Nikki let her approach. Rebecca's hand was soft on her arm, guiding, not grabbing. She allowed herself to be steered back to the door. Rebecca smiled kindly. Nikki pushed the wet hair out of her face. "Thanks for the clothes, um, Mrs....?"

"No need for that kind of formality." Rebecca turned to face Nikki. "Rebecca." The older woman held out her hand.

"Um, Nikki," she said as she took the woman's hand. Suddenly she was pulled into a hug. Nikki didn't know who instigated, but she was crying again. "Thank you so much. I...I...then Shane...and I..." she stuttered.

Rebecca rubbed Nikki's back. "Thank you for getting Shane here," she whispered. "We are so happy you both are here."

"I'm so sorry...I'm not..." Nikki tried to master her sobbing. "I'm sorry I'm not...Tammy...She's..." She was awash in tears. Rebecca held her close, her own tears streaming.

"We know. It is not your fault." Holding her at arm's length, Rebecca smiled at Nikki. "We are happy to have you. Any friend of Shane's…"

Nikki laughed through a sob. "I only just met him."

Rebecca held Nikki by the shoulders. "You have done more for him than anyone, including his father, ever did. You could have left him, dumped him on the side of the road. You are important and a true friend."

"He would have annoyed the hell out of me if I tried to dump him." Nikki smiled.

Rebecca laughed as she let Nikki go. "He only really annoys people he likes."

"Thanks." Nikki smiled as he opened the door to Shane's room.

"Hey, Nik," he muttered, trying to prop himself up.

"It's still Nikki, you big jerk." She turned back to Rebecca, rolling her eyes. "See." She sat on the edge of the bed. "Don't scare me like that again," she huffed. "Probably not even that injured. Just being overly dramatic."

"Well, you know how men are." Rebecca smiled. "They get the sniffles, it's the plague; get a cut, and it is a grievous wound. They are the human version of WebMD."

Alistair pushed past his wife with a tray of sandwiches and drinks. Nikki made an attempt to be polite but in the end, was overwhelmed by her desire to no longer feel hungry. A couple of helpings later found her dozing in a chair.

Alistair had asked what had happened to them. Nikki had told her story. It had been painful as she thought of Tim and her family and friends. When she came to the point where she had met Shane, she let him take over. Shane filled in the time before they met. He told of living in the woods since the dead began to walk, sleeping in caves and trees for days and seeing the dead from the outlying areas heading toward town. Shane's mood improved as he found out some of his family was still alive, even if they were basically trapped in some mansion. Nikki pretended to sleep when Alistair began to describe watching the end of the world. How it was happening everywhere. How scientists had no idea how it was spreading or even what had caused it. Now there was nothing on any satellite, broadband, Internet site, or radio wave with any news. The only contact they had was with the people downtown and the occasional shortwave radio operator.

Fire

"Keep the windows shut. Grab some more wet towels to block out the smoke," Gwen called. "Hayley, please move the children from the windows. We don't need them seeing that."

Hayley made no effort to usher the two children from the window. She was far too busy creating emergency packs in case they had to flee. Chris was the one to move them to a bedroom where Mary heard him suggest a game. She took their place at the glass. The air grew thicker with smoke throughout the day. They had no idea where the fire had started, only that it was progressing closer and closer.

Mary had agreed with Hayley. The wide main street with its median of trees and grass and two lanes on either side would stop the flames. She was sure they were safe from the flames, at least those that were torching the buildings. What she wasn't so sure of were the flames that wandered across Main Street. The flames had pushed the undead like an incoming tide ahead of it. Slowly at first, one or two; then it was a stream and then a flood. Mary was watching a shambling mass of death creeping ever closer, swirling and crashing against the foot of their sanctuary.

At first, they were simply the same as they had been seeing for days—torn and bloody remains of everyday life milling around the streets. As the fire grew closer, new arrivals smoldered over the roadway. They brought the smell of burning meat with them along with the smoke that blew in, obscuring the view ever so often.

A cloud of smoke cleared the street. Mary watched a zombie, with fire still clinging to its jacket, stumble and fall. It did not get back up. It was then she saw it—movement along the buildings.

"There's someone out there," Mary cried her face at the glass and hands gripping the coarse wooden frame tight.

"There are a lot of them out there. More coming every moment," Gwen replied, rushing past Mary.

"No shit. I mean living people are out there!" Mary exclaimed.

"There is no one alive out there. You are seeing things through the smoke and fire." Gwen didn't even bother to look. Hayley was by Mary's side. Mary was pointing along the building fronts. Hayley stared. Her shrug turned into a grip of Mary's arm.

"Zombies don't run." Hayley's words hung in the air for a second before everyone was crowded around the window. They watched three figures dart across the street, swinging various items and felling the undead as they ran.

"Gimme a flashlight or something!" Mary yelled, banging on the glass. "We need to get them to the building two over."

"Why there?" Chris asked from her shoulder.

"Because that is where we left those emergency supplies and the radio," Hayley explained.

Safe

Nikki pulled the knit hat lower over her ears as she pulled the sleeves up a little on the heavy winter coat. A light snow swirled and blew across the compound. The car she had driven in was covered from the last heavy snow. She blew into her hands before giving up against the cold. Retreating into the monitor room, she thanked the small space heater for its warmth. Peeling off the gloves, she flipped on the main viewer. She watched the six zombies that had gathered at the very front gate. There was no real change; they still meandered about, occasionally bumping into the fence. The cold did seem to slow them down a little. Becoming bored, she switched the feed to the one lone zombie that still wandered aimlessly through the fence line. It had made a long furrow in the snow but also could not hold her attention. The smell of hot chocolate met her nose, and she turned to see Shane emerge from the stairwell.

"Here, it's damn cold out there," he said, handing her the cup.

"'Bout time you got here. It *is* freakin' damn cold." She held the cup between her hands, reveling in the warmth.

"How's our friend?" he asked, pointing to the lone figure that had become very interested in its own tracks through the snow.

"Same as always—far from us," she said, handing Shane the binoculars as she headed for the door. "Have fun with the snow. I'm going to thaw out with a long shower."

"Alistair is making lasagna for dinner; don't want to miss that," he told her over his shoulder.

Nikki hesitated at the door. "Shane?"

"Yeah, Nik?"

She frowned, inhaled, and made the decision. "Thanks for getting me out of the tree," she softly replied, watching his shoulders sag slightly.

He turned to face her, a smile playing at the corner of his mouth. "Thanks for getting me here," he responded, letting the smile form.

She allowed one in return before she turned to go. The door opened, and she turned back. He waited. She looked him dead in the eye. "It's still Nikki."

Laughing, he waved her off with "Shhhh."

Time to Move

Ray stumbled to a stop as Dude Cat grouchily meowed, sweeping past him with a pink bow on his tail. Just past the man, Dude stopped and looked back into the room he had just left and gave an annoyed "Merrow." He eyed Ray, who held up his hands in a "What can I do?" The cat trotted off. Ray smiled and stepped into the room. He stumbled to a halt for the second time. His eyebrows shot up on their own with the tilt of his head.

"That's a good look," Ray commented to his son. Kyle's long hair was pulled back into a braid that ended in a pretty pink bow. Krissy was still fussing with the bow as her father walked by. Kyle looked up at his father but just shook his head, shrugged, and smiled. Ray gave the thumbs-up and returned to the hall. Snow fell heavily past the window. He watched it for a few minutes, remembering shoveling, driving on slippery roads, and scraping windows. What he wouldn't give to still have that to deal with. A long breath fogged up the cold glass. Ray continued on to the kitchen. Walking into the pantry, he grimaced at the shelves. Their supplies were starting to run low. Alistair had told them it was only set up for a few months, not for too extended of a stay—and not for four people. Jen appeared at his side, slipping her hand into his.

"We're still OK for a little while," she said, giving his hand a squeeze.

"But what then?" he asked, not really wanting to think about the answer. The prospect of leaving the house was one that no one wished to consider. Two weeks after they arrived, all the power had gone out in the city. The house on the left had caught fire and burned to the ground. Before the snow fell, the wind would still bring the burnt smell to them. They could see the dead wandering the streets. With each day there seemed to be more and more of them arriving. They wandered aimlessly outside the wall. It was as if they knew there were people alive there.

"Well, let's see if Alistair has an idea," Jen finally answered, doubt betrayed by her voice. She left the pantry, and Ray followed.

Ray paused his collecting of dinner items. He knew she was worried; so was he. Shaking his worry, he headed back into the kitchen to start making dinner. Jen stood at the counter, staring at nothing. "An idea? Like what?" Ray asked his wife.

Jen's eyes and shrug told Ray she didn't have a clue. Instead of an answer, she proceeded to get out a pot to help.

"Sorry," Ray grumbled.

Jen placed a hand on his arm and gave it a squeeze. "We're going to be OK. I promise."

Kyle noticed the dinners getting smaller over the next couple of weeks but said nothing. Krissy just complained that they never had pizza. Ray noticed that Kyle's portions seemed smaller than what was given him, and Krissy's were always more. Kyle and Ray caught each other's eyes. Kyle's head gave a slight tilt and Ray a slight nod. They had an agreement.

Ray had spoken with Alistair several times, but he didn't mention the dwindling supplies. He didn't want to know that there was no backup plan. It was clear that whatever Alistair had planned for this place, it wasn't for a zombie takeover. Every day the knot in his stomach grew tighter. He wandered outside and was trudging through the snow toward the gate. He could hear the moans of the undead just over the wall. He wondered how many were out there now. The Volvo and Camaro were both covered in snow. He stood staring at the white mounds encasing the vehicles, wondering which would be the smarter one to use to escape the zombies.

"Hey, Dad, if we are gonna make a run for it, I suggest the Camaro." Ray jumped at the sound of his son's voice. He had been so deep in thought that he didn't even hear him approach. "You better learn to be more observant, or a zombie is gonna bite your ass off." Kyle laughed.

"Nice. Watch your language," Ray answered, distracted. He walked up to the gate and then turned back to his son. "Why the Camaro?"

Kyle walked past his father and slid the cover to the small observation port open. He immediately jumped back as a face of a zombie was looking in from the other side. Slamming the cover shut, he exclaimed, "Shit! Ugly fucker. Um, well, because the Camaro has a bigger engine. We can go faster and, if we need to, plow right through 'em."

Ray studied Kyle for a moment. "Yeah, but the Volvo has a better safety rating. If we crash, there is a better chance of getting out OK."

Kyle pondered this for a moment. "That is a good point." Ray took a step back, holding his heart. Kyle frowned. "Funny, you know, we could take both." Ray's hand went up to protest. "No, wait, listen." Ray's hand hovered and then fell as Kyle continued, "We slam through with the Camaro and use the Volvo to get Mom and Krissy out."

The crunch of snow alerted them to Jen's appearance. "Or we could listen to the idea Alistair has." She eyed both men with the look only a wife and mother could give to note her disapproval.

"We were just discussing the merits of the vehicles," Ray began.

"Yeah, just hypothetically, Mom," Kyle finished.

"Get in the house, both of you. Alistair wants to talk to us." Jen turned on her heels and marched back to the house.

Kyle bent over quickly, packing snow. Hefting the snowball, he began to aim at his mother. Ray cleared his throat and shook his head, a deep frown on his face. Disappointed, Kyle nodded and dropped the missile. He had just started to follow his mother when his own snowball hit him square in the back. After a few frantic minutes of snowballs flying across the yard, a very annoyed Jen retrieved her family.

A Plan

Alistair began to get annoyed. He had been staring at the empty living room for the last five minutes. He started grumbling about courtesy when Rebecca walked in and laughed.

"Someplace you have to be?" she asked.

Alistair looked up at her and shook his head. "This is important." He took a drink and looked at the glass. "I never planned to have that place occupied very long. We didn't get a chance to outfit it correctly."

"I know, I know," she soothed. "This is very important, and they will be very thankful." She took a seat next to him.

Looking over her shoulder, he asked, "Where are the kids?" He was more looking for something to do while waiting for his sister-in-law and her family to show up than really concerned.

"They are up in the tower. Are you going to take Shane with you?" Rebecca studied her husband.

"If he wants to go." He shrugged.

"What about Nikki?" She crossed her arms, waiting for an answer.

He was saved from answering as the family appeared on the screen. Alistair frowned, noting the look of a snowball fight that covered three members.

"They were messing around outside," Krissy informed her uncle.

"I see that," he answered, trying but failing to leave the annoyance out of his voice.

"What is going on?" Ray answered, with the same tone in his voice. Alistair and Ray stared at each other for a moment.

"How are you holding up?" Rebecca finally broke the staring contest. "How are...things?"

"If you are talking about the supplies, we are starting to get a little concerned," Jen told her sister.

"I never planned to stay at that location longer than a month or two. You will be running out of fuel and food before too much longer." Alistair sighed.

Krissy gave a small yelp. Ray put his hands on his daughter's shoulders and gave her a reassuring hug. "I don't want to go back out there," Krissy whispered while looking up at her father.

Alistair smiled at her. "Don't worry; I'll be coming to get you."

Ray and Kyle looked at each other. Ray started to speak, but Kyle beat him to it. "In what?" Kyle lowered his voice slightly. "Uncle Alistair, this place is seriously surrounded." Kyle glanced at his sister before moving even closer to the monitor. "Last time we looked, they were like three deep."

Alistair nodded; rubbing his chin, he smiled. "I have a vehicle that will do the job nicely. There is only a small issue of getting through the gate," Alistair stated. He then proceeded to outline his plan to get the family from the house in the city to his bunker in the woods. "OK, so it is decided. As long as the weather holds, I'll be there in two days. That will give you time to collect your stuff and for us to prepare." Alistair paused and added, "If we get too much more snow, we may have to delay. I know, I know! I don't like it either!" he exclaimed over several protests. "If we have too much, it could leave us in big trouble. Trust me, I will get you as soon as possible."

Need to Take a Trip into Town

Nikki entered the kitchen and inhaled deeply. The delicious smell filled her nose. Alistair was just bringing the lasagna out onto the table. She closed her eyes and thought of her grandmother for a moment. A picture of her family flickered across her mind. Grief filled her for a moment but was pushed from her mind as she herself was pushed by Shane.

"Quit blocking the door, Nik." He laughed.

"Nikki!" She swatted him.

"Sit," Rebecca admonished, brandishing a salad spoon.

"Where did you get the lettuce?" Nikki asked, scooting her chair in.

"Hydroponics," Shane answered. "You just now thought to ask?"

"I want to talk to you about something," Alistair interrupted, heading off the verbal altercation he could see coming. "I need to go into the city to get Ray, Jen, and the kids. I could use your help." His attention was on his nephew.

"No problem," Nikki stated, looking down to cut her lasagna.

Alistair turned his attention from Shane to Nikki. He had not expected her to volunteer. She looked up and around the table at all the staring faces. "What?" she asked.

"Well, I just thought you...um would stay behind." Alistair shrugged.

"Why? Because I'm a girl? I think I did a damn good job getting here," she fired up at once.

"Nikki, chill. I'm sure he didn't mean anything by it," Shane defended.

She turned to Shane, confused. "Did you just tell me to chill?"

Shane shrugged at her, turning his attention back to Alistair. "So, Unc, when do we leave?" he asked, digging into his own dinner.

"Day after tomorrow."

"How are we getting there?" Nikki inquired while grabbing a slice of bread, slapping Shane's hand out of the way. He threw a cucumber slice at her.

"I've got a Bradley Fighting Vehicle," Alistair replied, rubbing his temple and ignoring a cherry tomato flying across the table.

"*No way!*" Shane exclaimed, knocking the tomato away. "It is kind of like a tank," he explained, noting the look of confusion on Nikki's face. Rebecca cleared her throat, and Shane dropped the butter pad he was aiming at Nikki. She stuck her tongue out at him. Rebecca pointed at her with the same look she had just given Shane.

Alistair kept ignoring the interactions. "I have the M242 and the M240c on it. They should provide enough firepower." He rolled his eyes at Rebecca. "This," he pointed between Nikki and Shane, "is why I never wanted children!"

"A chain gun and a machine gun," Shane explained. "The 242 has a dual feed that the gunner can switch between armor-piercing or high-explosive rounds. The 240 machine gun fires 7.622 mm rounds." Noticing Nikki still looked confused, he added, "I had been planning on joining the army at one time."

"Well, we should be well protected. Are you coming, Rebecca?" Nikki asked.

"With both of you going"—Rebecca ignored the grunt of protest from her husband—"I don't need to."

"Rebecca, you know the systems already. I would rather you go," Alistair began.

"Yes, but I also know the defenses of the compound better," she stated simply.

"Wait a minute," Shane exclaimed while slowly letting his fork down to the plate. "Nikki and I have explored this whole compound. Where are you hiding this beast?"

Nikki looked up at Alistair. What Shane had said was true. The house was huge, almost like a hotel. It had ten bedrooms, each with its own bathroom. The basement was a labyrinth of storerooms and equipment. There were water purifiers; geothermal heating, solar, and wind transformers; and all kinds of things that neither Nikki nor Shane understood. They had found the huge generator room and even the garbage room, but they had never found a garage.

Alistair smiled and took a bite of his dinner. Looking thoughtfully between them, he took a sip of wine and then wiped his mouth. "You have only been in about half of the compound." He smiled again. "There is a door in the back of storeroom three that leads to a tunnel. If the compound were ever breached, we could live in the underground bunker for several years without problems." He enjoyed the effect this had on them. "The garage is off one of the tunnels." He took a slice of bread and began to mop up some of the sauce from his plate.

Nikki looked over at Shane, who wore the same stunned expression.

Getting Ready to Go

Krissy held her brother's hand as their parents explained the situation. Their uncle would be coming tomorrow to get them. They had to pack up their belongings and be ready to go by noon the next day.

Kyle smiled down at Krissy. "Hey, don't worry," he whispered. "Mom and Dad will make sure we are safe, and Uncle Al had this place." He gestured around. "It kept us really protected. So you know the place we are going has got to be even better." She nodded; he could tell she wasn't quite convinced. She just looked up at her brother and tried to believe that everything was going to be OK. Inside she was terrified to go back past the gates. She had been playing on the wall, throwing snowballs at the zombies when she saw a boy among them. This boy had been one of her friends. They had played together at school. She hadn't left the house since seeing him.

Krissy returned to her room and stared at her few possessions. She had some clothes and a few toys. There was a spoon man Kyle had made her because, as he put it, her doll needed a friend. She picked up the spoon man and began to halfheartedly play with it and her doll.

"Once we get to your uncle's, we will not have to leave again," Ray spoke from her doorway. She only nodded but did not answer.

Kyle walked up behind his father. "She is really scared to go back out there," he whispered. "I guess seeing someone you knew…"

Ray turned to his son. "Promise me you'll take care of her. Don't let anything happen to her, and promise me you'll be careful," he said, pulling Kyle into a hug.

Kyle stood rigid and stunned for a second before returning the hug. "Get it together, Dad. We're gonna be fine. You take care of Mom, and I'll take care of Kris." He held his father at arm's length. "Deal?"

"Deal." Ray nodded.

Prep Time

Nikki and Shane followed Alistair through the door in the back of the storeroom. He flipped a switch, and the fluorescent lights flickered to life. They were standing in a long, white tunnel. As they proceeded, Shane noticed they were walking down a slope. Every so often Alistair would open a heavy metal door segmenting the tunnel.

"Just in case," Alistair said as Shane gave him a questioning look about the doors.

"Seriously paranoid," Nikki whispered. Shane laughed while Alistair ignored her.

They came to another door; this one had a keypad by it. Alistair punched in a code and pushed the door open. Cool, damp air rushed into the tunnel. Alistair stepped forward into the dark room and disappeared for a moment. Lights hummed and bathed the room in light.

Shane stepped through the door and gave a low whistle. A cavernous garage containing several vehicles met his gaze. There was a huge tour bus–type RV, several very expensive sports cars, a Bentley, and...

"That is a tank!" Nikki gasped. "A freaking tank." She was pointing.

"No, it is an armored personnel carrier." Shane grabbed her arm, pulling her along behind him. "See here." He pointed to the rear of the vehicle. "The back opens to allow troops to exit quickly while the guns provide fire support," he stated.

"It's got...tank wheels," she stuttered. "I mean tracks."

"Tread," Shane corrected.

Alistair stepped up to the back of the vehicle. "OK, let's go over this again." Nikki and Shane listened carefully. "We back up to the gate; Shane, you will man the guns blowing away any of the ghouls who come too close." Shane saluted. "Nikki, you'll cover the family from the back." She gave a thumbs-up. "In and out in five minutes. The whole trip shouldn't take more than two hours," he concluded.

They spent the next couple of hours going over the weapons system, how to drive the vehicle, operating the rear gate, and loading and checking their personal weapons. Nikki was somewhat intimidated by the efficiency of Alistair and Shane at the loading and cleaning of the weapons.

After what felt like hours of going over and over what they were going to do and how all the systems worked, Alistair finally let them go. The plan was for them to leave at first light the next morning, so everyone retired early. Nikki stared into the void of the blackness of her room. The silence pressed on her ears. Sleep finally overtook her, but rest was not to be found. She was back in the restaurant. Tim was eating a little girl while a waitress, covered in blood and missing a hand, was asking for her drink order. Nikki turned at a tap on her shoulder to find a zombie Shane trying to bite into her arm. The scene dissolved into a cross between the thrift shop and the convenience store. Zombies were eating her friends while trying on sunglasses. Something pulled at her arm. It was a dead Shane, his teeth poised to sink into her arm. Before she could pull it away, they were back in the cabin. The undead Shane advanced on her. She held up her arm in defense, his teeth ripping into the soft flesh. Nikki woke up, rolling off her arms. They stung of pins and needles while her hair stuck to her face on the soaking pillow. She could still see his twisted face burned into her eyelids. Nikki did not return to sleep. The knock at the door calling her to get ready was a welcome one.

Time to Go...Again

Ray, Jen, Kyle, and Krissy spent the morning collecting their possessions. A light snow had begun to fall. Ray checked his watch. They would be leaving by 11:00 a.m. and Ray knew his family was anxious. The group of zombies outside the wall seemed to sense the family's activity. When Ray and Kyle had surveyed the surroundings, it seemed as if their number had doubled overnight. Jen and Ray were busy moving the few items to the gate while Kyle kept Krissy distracted. Every time he left her on her own, she would start to get upset to the point of hysterics. Kyle had taken it upon himself to take care of his sister, seeing how anxious his parents were becoming. Jen had taken over while Ray pulled Kyle aside.

"I know you are going to keep her safe," Ray whispered. "If this goes wrong, if Jen and I don't..."

"Dad, we are all going to be fine. Uncle Al is coming to get us," Kyle interrupted, not wishing to even think about what Ray was saying.

"I know, I know, but if...we get separated," Ray inhaled, "you and your sister are to get out of town. Head west. There will be fewer people out that way. Promise me you will keep her safe."

"Dad, I already promised that." Kyle placed a hand on his father's shoulder. "We are all getting out of this...together." He held Ray's gaze for a moment. Looking over the older man's shoulder, Kyle called. "Kris, Dad was just saying we need to find something to carry Dude in."

The next few minutes were spent trying to locate and then capture an increasingly annoyed Dude. It appeared he still remembered Krissy's bow and wasn't too keen on another fashion accessory. The makeshift cat carrier did nothing to calm his mood.

On the Road

The lack of sleep vanished the moment Nikki stepped into the armored steel machine. She sat in the front next to Alistair. Shane was already up in the turret. Alistair reached up and clicked the small black button attached to the sun visor. Not sure what she had expected, Nikki found that the sound of the heavy door rolling back surprised her. Her hand flew to cover her eyes. She was blinded momentarily as the sunlight blazed through the front windows. Snow left fat, wet flakes on the glass as the armored car pulled forward.

This was the first time in two months Nikki had left the safety of the compound. It was freeing and terrifying at once. The feel of heavy steel calmed her nerves slightly. Making her way to the back, she looked out through the tiny portal to watch the door shut. It was camouflaged to match the hillside. Even through her anxiety at leaving and the excitement of the task ahead, she had to shake her head at Alistair's efforts. "Seriously paranoid." She laughed to herself. "Thank God."

Shane appeared at her side. He laughed at her reaction. "Yep, just like the Batcave." Alistair nodded at Shane's call.

"Yeah, batshit crazy, man," Nikki teased, earning her a swat from Shane.

They wound their way down what might have been a dirt road when it wasn't snow-covered. "I wish it was snowing harder. I don't like leaving tracks," Alistair grumbled. Meeting up with a snow-covered, paved road, Alistair urged more speed out of the vehicle. With the increased speed came the increased butterflies, making Nikki wish she had only had the coffee for breakfast.

A few miles from the compound, they met their first zombies. Three of them wandered around on the road a short distance from the wreck of a car.

"Looks like they might have been a family...once," Shane noted, pulling back the action on the main fifty-caliber gun, ready to fire as they passed the ghouls. Alistair didn't even flinch when they ran over what had once been a young boy. The other two lumbered after the Bradley for a little while, not even noticing that one of their numbers was no longer moving.

The closer they got to town, the more wrecked cars and undead they encountered. Alistair slowed the Bradley as they entered the outskirts of town. They passed empty houses. Everything was covered in pristine, untouched snow. Nikki thought it would be very pretty if it weren't so eerie. Normally there would be the buzz of snow throwers mixed with the scrape of snow shovels. The white blanket hid the scarred lawns torn by speeding tires and bloodstained pavement, and signs of violence disappeared under the smooth cover. The fact that nothing was disturbed bothered Nikki. Since they had entered the suburbs, they had not seen one single zombie. On top of that, there didn't seem to be any evidence of them. Not a single track in the snow. Alistair drove slowly, stopping on occasion, hoping to coax out any survivors. Faces never appeared in the windows, and no doors opened. There was simply no one around. After Shane let the fifty bark off several rounds with still no sign of life (or death), they continued on. Finally, Alistair stopped at a bridge spanning the frozen river that led into the heart of the city.

"The house is on the other side of town," he said, glancing at his watch. "We should be right on time, barring any detours." Putting the vehicle in low gear, he proceeded to drive up and over the pile of cars blocking the bridge.

Nikki bounced around the back as they crested the smashed vehicles. "Warn me next time!" she shouted, rubbing her butt that she had just been knocked on.

Shane looked back and shouted over the engine, "Buckle up for safety." She gave him the finger in return. He laughed, but she could see the tension in his smile.

Unexpected Detour

"Shit! We're not getting through that!" Shane exclaimed as Alistair stopped the Bradley. Nikki was at Alistair's shoulder, looking out in front of the vehicle. The way was blocked. The building on the left had apparently caught fire and collapsed onto the road, taking part of the building across the street with it.

"Looks like we're going to have to go around." Alistair began to shift the mighty vehicle in reverse. "Oh, hello!" he exclaimed as several zombies stumbled out of a building next to the Bradley.

Nikki returned to the back and looked out the small port. "We have more friends behind us," she stated while sitting quickly and buckling her seat belt. She had a feeling things were about to get bumpy. Nikki's head swung side to side as dull thumps began to sound through the armor as the undead tried to get at the living.

Alistair slammed the vehicle in reverse. Watching the display, he backed the vehicle over several of the zombies. Nikki cringed as she heard them hit the door next to her and get crunched under the tread. Reaching the cross street, Alistair put the Bradley back into gear. Returning his gaze to the front, he swore. The street was full of shambling horror. Shane moved to return to the turret but was stopped by his uncle.

The pounding intensified as the Bradley just sat there. More and more zombies crowded around the armored car. Shane looked over at his uncle, who still had a hand on Shane's arm, keeping him in his seat.

Nikki covered her ears as the drumming on the side got louder and louder. "Why aren't we moving?" she cried, unable to keep the panic out of her voice.

"What's up, Uncle?" Shane whispered. He was starting to get concerned. Alistair pointed up the street. Hanging out a window was a person frantically waving a flag.

"I don't think zombies are that patriotic," Alistair stated.

"What is going on?" Nikki screamed. Clawed hands left black streaks on the portal. The Bradley was starting to shake.

"There is someone up ahead, alive. We are drawing the zombies to us; then we'll leave them here and get the survivor!" Shane shouted back.

Alistair poked Shane and then pointed his thumb up to the turret. Shane nodded and opened the hatch. The cold flooded down over Nikki, bringing with it the stench of the dead. She covered her ears as the main gun opened up on the road in front of the Bradley. The clang of spent brass shells banged off the roof of the vehicle.

Alistair waited until an area of about a hundred feet in front of the survivor's building was clear before proceeding forward. Shane spun the gun to cover the rear of the Bradley. The survivor ducked into the building as the vehicle trundled closer, finally coming to a halt in front of the sanctuary as a rope ladder fell from a second-floor window and four heavily bundled people began their descent.

"Around the back!" Shane shouted to the group. Yelling into the compartment of the Bradley, he added, "Nikki, open the gate!" She punched the seat-belt release and sprang to her feet, hitting the button to lower the rear gate. The cold slapped her in the face as snow swirled into the warm interior. The rear gate was three quarters down when Shane opened fire again. Nikki could see the horde they had just left starting to advance toward them.

The last of the four was on the ladder. "Come on!" the one in the front turned and shouted and then screamed as the straggler fell from the ladder with a thump into the snow. Staggering to her feet, she ran to catch up. The one in the front was pulling a smaller one by the hand.

Nikki held onto a handle just inside the gate and reached out to help them aboard. The gate was almost down when the small form was thrust at Nikki. With her free hand, Nikki pulled what she could only assume was a child on board. The leader then clambered in and turned to encourage the last two on. The one who fell from the ladder stumbled and fell again. Nikki could see the eyes of the person who was almost at the safety of the fighting vehicle. She could see the terror and the conflict. The person stopped, spun around, and ran back. Sliding in the snow, she grabbed the fallen person. Picking him up out of the snow, she placed him hard on his feet. The fallen boy nodded and allowed himself to be pulled to the Bradley.

Shane opened up with the machine gun again. Nikki could hear the moans of the dead and smell the stench over the blowing snow and the cordite from the firing gun. "Is this it? Is this everyone?" Nikki yelled at the bundled newcomers. The first one who had made it inside stared around at the others.

"Yes, four of us" came the muffled reply.

"All in, Alistair!" Nikki cried, hitting the button to close the gate. The vehicle lurched forward. Nikki watched the dead hurry after them until the gate clanged shut. Nikki swung into her seat and was pressed into the side as Alistair took a corner. Shane stumbled down the ladder and slammed the hatch. Snow drifted to the floor and melted; the sound of labored breathing filled the space. Slowly the air began to warm with the heater going and the portals all closed.

"What do we got?" Alistair questioned from the driver's seat.

"We got four newbies, Unc," Shane shouted, steadying himself as Alistair took another corner.

Nikki's hand was inside her jacket, fingering the handle of her gun. She watched the four newcomers. They were looking around the interior with frightened interest. They huddled close together. All Nikki could see of them were their eyes under the heavy winter clothes.

Finally, one of them reached up and began to pull off some of the scarves and hats that covered her head. Shane stepped forward and sat next to Nikki as the woman got up off the floor and sat in the seat across from them. Taking their cue, the others moved to the seats next to the woman and pulled off their own hats and scarves. Seated across from Nikki and Shane sat a woman with short, spiky, reddish-brown hair. Nikki judged her to be around Shane's age. Judging by the way Shane reacted, so did he. Nikki frowned.

Next to the woman sat a young boy of about ten. He had unkempt blond hair. A young woman sat next to the boy. She had her arm around him. His eyes were filled with fear as he nuzzled against the girl. Nikki recognized the girl's blue eyes; she was the one who had gone back for the boy. Nikki had an immediate dislike for her that she couldn't explain. The girl had brown roots showing from a black dye job that had grown out. In the black dye, there were purple streaks. The girl pulled off her gloves, and as Nikki suspected, she saw chipped black fingernail polish.

Nikki's attention was pulled from the girl as a young man with the same dazzling blue eyes pulled off his hat and scarves. Nikki smiled at him; he returned it. Both Shane and the black-haired girl frowned. The young boy whimpered.

"Easy, Squeaker." The girl spoke in a soothing voice.

"Hello, I'm Shane, and this is my friend Nikki." Shane's jovialness broke the silence.

Nikki frowned again as she heard Shane emphasize "friend." It wasn't as if she was interested in him, but did he have to be so blatant? *Seriously! We are on a rescue mission in a city of the dead. Calm your raging hormones,* she thought.

The woman with spiky hair looked over at Shane. "Thank you so much for stopping. My name is Hayley. This is Chris." She gestured to the young man, who nodded at both of them. His eye lingered on Nikki, and he smiled. She smiled back; he was kinda cute. Before Nikki could chastise herself for acting like Shane, Hayley continued, "That is his sister Mary."

Mary gave a noncommittal acknowledgment. Nikki returned it with a feeling of satisfaction that she was just as Nikki expected her to be and also Chris's sister. Mentally slapping herself, Nikki turned to the young boy. "Hi, what is your name?" The boy shuffled closer to Mary.

"We call him Squeaker. He doesn't speak, so we don't know his real name," Mary huffed.

"I ran into these two about a week after it all started. We picked up Squeaker a few days later. There were more of us at first. We were holed up in an apartment house at first, but they got in," Hayley explained.

"Do you know of any other survivors?" Alistair called from the front.

"There was this couple we were talking to on these two-way radios," Chris explained, pulling a radio out of his pocket, "but we haven't heard from them in a week or so."

"Why do you still have that?" Mary hissed at her brother.

"Let it go, Mare," he glowered back.

"Mare?" Shane questioned.

"Probably short for Nightmare," Nikki whispered as she rolled her eyes.

Mary looked over with a sneer. "Not all of us could be cheerleaders."

"I was never a cheerleader!" Nikki shot back.

"Does it matter?" Chris jumped in. "Seriously!"

Shane caught Hayley's eye and smiled.

"We haven't seen anyone else alive in weeks," Hayley spoke up, trying to calm the tension. "You guys aren't the army, so who are you?"

Shane and Nikki explained about Alistair and how they had ended up at his house in the woods.

"So you were hiding in the attic above the convenience store over on Fernwood?" Chris asked Nikki. "Did you go to Glendale?"

"Yeah, where did you go?"

"Forest Hills." He smiled. Mary just shuffled in her seat and glared at the floor.

Nikki laughed to herself. Forest Hills had been the "rich kids'" school. *Typical*, she thought.

"So you just drive through the city looking for survivors?" Hayley asked. Shane explained the reason for their trip from the safety of the compound.

"Alistair, where are you? Ray just called, and they are still waiting," Rebecca's voice crackled over the radio.

"We got sidetracked and picked up four more friends," Alistair replied into the handset.

"Are they all OK?" Rebecca asked. Alistair turned and gave Shane a look. Shane nodded and stood up.

Where Are They?

Ray trudged back out to his waiting family. The wind and the zombies howled. The snow had begun to fall fast and heavy. Dude scratched at the inside of the cardboard box Krissy and Kyle had forced him into.

"Are they coming?" Jen asked her husband. Pounding met their ears as the zombies behind the gate heard her words. Krissy clung tightly to her brother.

"Rebecca says they got detoured on the way here and found some other survivors. They are over on Moknocker drive now," Ray shouted over the wind and moans.

"Moknocker? That is at least twenty minutes away. We should go back in and let them calm down." Kyle motioned to the gate. Ray nodded. It was best to let the zombies forget why they were so interested in the gate. Jen picked up Dude's box, but the cat shifted and she lost her grip. The box tumbled from her hands and Dude ran free.

Krissy's cry gave way to a laugh as the cat jumped up, hopping around in the deep snow. Kyle ran after the animal. Ray followed, trying to wrangle the flailing cat. Kyle gave a spectacular dive. The air was full of flying snow and howling cat. Clutching his pet to his chest, Kyle rolled over in the snow, shushing the meowing cat.

"Shh, Dude, shh. They'll hear you," Kyle cooed.

Krissy's laugh died in her throat as the pounding on the gate and the moans from over the wall intensified. Ray ran to his daughter as her head spun from left to right, looking for an escape. Wrapping his arms around the struggling girl as she panicked and tried to run for the house, Ray looked through the blowing snow at Kyle as each struggled with his charge.

"Krissy, Krissy!" Kyle yelled. "I need your help with Dude."

She whimpered in her father's arms. Jen knelt down beside her. "Honey, your brother needs your help with Dude Cat. Can you help him?" Krissy looked over at her brother as he struggled with the small cat. Krissy nodded. Ray held her hand as she slowly approached Kyle. He held out the cat to her. Dude seemed to resign himself to be held and allowed Krissy to take him from Kyle.

Struggling to his feet in the deep snow and wind, Kyle checked his watch. "Well, that killed some time. I don't expect there to be much traffic, so Uncle Alistair should be along anytime."

More Than Expected

Shane looked over at the four newcomers and then gave Nikki a significant look. "Is everyone OK? Anyone hurt or bitten?" he asked.

Hayley's head turned quickly, her eyes searching his. "No one has been bitten. We know what happens to those who have been bitten."

Shane looked over at Mary. "Are you OK? You seemed to have some trouble." Mary glared at him.

"She is just a klutz, and she always skipped gym," Chris defended.

Nikki laughed. Mary's glare turned to her immediately. "Relax; I hated gym, too." Nikki smiled. Mary, in spite of herself, smiled back.

"So you are OK?" Shane asked Mary.

"I hurt my ankle falling off the ladder. Thanks for pointing it out," she grumbled. Shane toppled backward and grabbed the handrail on the ceiling for support as the Bradley lurched to a stop.

"Shane, Nikki!" Alistair called from the front. Nikki, Shane, and Hayley all rushed to him. Through the wipers brushing the fast-falling snow, they saw what caused Alistair to stop.

"Oh my God," Shane whispered.

"How are you going to get through that?" Hayley breathed.

Through the swirling snow, they could see the high walls of Alistair's downtown compound—the walls that Ray and his family were waiting behind. Before them was a sea of the undead. They seemed like a school of sharks circling the perimeter.

"It's like they know there is food in there," Hayley spoke. "Just like when we were in the apartment—just one or two at first. We thought they would go away once they knew they couldn't get in, but the longer we were there, the more would come."

"Nothing attracts a crowd like a crowd," Alistair commented. "It's pack mentality, I think."

"Whatever it is, that is a shitload of zombies!" Shane pointed out.

"And behind that shitload is our family. Family we are not leaving here!" Alistair replied angrily.

"Never suggested any different, Uncle. Just need a better plan than charging straight in," Shane defended, holding up his hands.

"Why not do what we did back at Hayley's place?" Nikki asked.

"That did seem to work rather well," Hayley agreed.

Arrival

Krissy screamed and Dude yowled as several explosions echoed outside the high walls. Kyle ran to the gate, throwing open the portal. Instead of the usual dead eyes glaring back, confusion met his gaze. Kyle ducked as several more explosions sounded outside. Dirt and debris flew through the hole.

"I think Uncle Alistair is here!" he yelled, wiping dirt and some blood from his face. Several scratches from flying rocks welled up. Krissy cried and squeezed Dude. Jen pulled the cat from her daughter, and Krissy grabbed her father's arm and crushed it. The family ducked as more rounds hit the crowd, and the gate rattled. Kyle returned to the lookout. "They are moving off. They are going after the...the...tank thing he is in!" Kyle cried.

***

"Jesus! They just keep coming!" Shane called out as he reloaded the gun. He fired several more rounds into the horde as they swelled forward.

Alistair and Hayley watched the zombies moving toward their position. "It doesn't look like we are going to get as a clear shot as we did with you." Alistair looked over at Hayley. Her face was pale, and her hands shook. Alistair reached out and placed a hand on hers. "I didn't get you out of there to let you die over here. We will get out of this, all of us," he reassured her.

Nikki pushed up another ammo box to Shane as he reloaded the main gun again. The Bradley shook, and the shell casings clanked over the side. Nikki now knew why they called the young boy Squeaker. He was huddled under his seat, covering his ears and making squeaking, whimpering noises. Mary was right beside him, whispering comfort to him. Nikki decided the girl couldn't be too bad if she went out of her way to comfort a scared child.

***

Kyle watched as the zombies thinned outside the gate. "They are going to run out of ammo before we run out of zombies," he noted as he reached into his coat and pulled out a gun. Placing the barrel through the opening, he fired.

"Kyle, don't!" Ray yelled. "Let them be distracted by one commotion!"

Kyle looked back out the portal and knew his father was right. Several of the undead had stopped moving off and were now approaching the gate. Kyle slammed the peephole shut and backed away. "Yeah, that is a good plan, Dad." Ray shook his head.

***

"This looks as good as we are gonna get!" Shane called as a mass of zombies approached through the billowing snow.

The walls were still surrounded by hundreds of ghouls even as the mass began to reach the armored car. Shane had changed over to his handgun as hands began to beat on the side of the vehicle. Mary's face was hidden as she comforted the scared boy. Chris's eyes again darted all over the interior as the thousands of fists beat and began to rock the heavy car.

Nikki moved over to Chris and held his hand. "It is gonna be fine. I promise."

"You better be right." Mary stared up at Nikki.

"Listen, it looks like I could use your help," Nikki explained.

"What can we do?" Chris asked, trying to appear braver than he felt.

***

"They're coming!" Kyle yelled.

Ray handed his daughter to Jen, who now had both the struggling cat and the terrified girl to contend with. The look she gave her husband told him he was asking a lot.

"Kyle, collect your sister or your cat," Ray called as he moved forward to the mechanism that held the gate shut.

Kyle grabbed the box that had once held Dude. He collected the cat. "It's only for a little bit, man. Relax." Dude meowed at him and allowed himself to be shut in the box. Kyle then grabbed his sister's hand.

Krissy cried freely next to him. "I don't wanna go. I don't wanna…I don't wanna play with Billy."

"You won't have to. Uncle Alistair is coming, and you'll meet some new friends," Kyle assured her. A rumble outside the gate and gunfire announced the arrival of Uncle Alistair.

Departure

"Ray! Open the gate!" Alistair's voice boomed over a loudspeaker. Ray struggled with the bolts. Jen strained next to him. They fell into the snow as the mechanism gave. Scrambling to their feet, they began to pull the gate back.

"Get ready, Krissy; time to go." Kyle squeezed her hand. Tears still ran freely down her face. The gate slid back, and the rear of the armored car pushed into the opening. The roof scraped on the top of the wall. Shane was firing all around the front and sides of the Bradley.

It was a tight fit, but not tight enough. On the left side, there was enough space for..."They're getting in!" Kyle screamed and reached for his gun. Krissy screamed and ran toward the house.

Kyle fired, and the first zombie fell. Behind, four more had entered the courtyard. Kyle caught sight of black-and-purple hair flying past him. Another girl was shooting at the other zombies in the yard.

Nikki fired another round and screamed at the two adults, "Get into the car!"

Jen and Ray grabbed their few belongings as Chris ran forward, grabbing what he could and throwing it into the back of the Bradley. He lost his grip on an oddly balanced box and jumped as a cat emerged and darted past him into the back of the vehicle. Once inside, Dude howled out to the family as if to call them to the safety.

"Krissy! Krissy!" Kyle screamed, scanning the courtyard for his sister as more zombies clawed past the vehicle.

Jen was in the back, calling out for her children. Nikki swore loudly and threw her empty gun at a zombie and ran while she pulled out another gun.

Ray grabbed Kyle and tried to pull him to the open door. A zombie lurched forward, trying to grab the men. Kyle smashed it upside the head with his empty gun. He lost his footing, falling in deep snow. Ray was pulling him through the snow now. Jen was being restrained by Hayley and Chris while she screamed for her family.

"I've got her! I've got her!" Mary called as she ran past with a struggling Krissy, who was flailing her arms and legs, trying to hit every inch of Mary she could. Mary threw the struggling girl into the back of the vehicle as Kyle struggled to his feet. Now he was pushing Ray forward.

Nikki was cut off, stuck behind several zombies that were between her and her escape. She fired several more rounds, and the slide slammed back. The clip was empty. Frantically she searched her pockets. The only weapon she had left was the knife Shane gave her.

The closest zombie dropped. Kyle ran forward; everyone in the back of the car was screaming. The zombies seemed confused. Several went for the two in the snow; several others tried to get at the closing door of the rescue vehicle.

Kyle grabbed Nikki's arm, and they ran toward the car. Kyle was ahead and elbowed a zombie out of the way. It spun comically on the spot, but then its hand caught the collar of Nikki's coat. She gagged as it cut into her throat. Her legs flew out from under her in the snow and she landed hard on her back. Nikki gasped for breath, trying to get to her feet as the zombie that had grabbed her hit the ground next to her.

She could smell its decay as it rolled over to face her. Nikki screamed. It moved over her. An eye hung from its socket; greenish yellow teeth hung from blackened gums. An ear hung from a flap of gray skin that was barely attached to its skull. Three fingers and a thumb reached for her as she flung up an arm. The zombie sunk its teeth into the down filling of the jacket. The tearing of the material filled her ears.

Screaming, she flung her other hand out and hit the zombie. Undeterred, it tried to bite at her again, but she was sliding quickly away. The zombie followed its prey with white, dead eyes, and then its skull exploded in gray and black. Nikki looked up as Shane pulled her by her jacket and fired at the closing zombies.

She was in the air and hit the floor of the Bradley hard; her arm exploded in pain. Shane hit the ground next to her. The interior darkened as the door shut. The floor rumbled, and the machine gun blared as they pulled away.

"Oh God, *oh God*! I've been bit!" Nikki wailed. She tried to pull off her coat, but the pain in her arm sent stars before her eyes, and she felt as if she would be sick. She looked up at Shane's stricken face as he pulled a knife. This was it. Her friend, the one she had made it to safety with, the one she had survived with, would be the one to end her life. It seemed fitting. Tears streamed down her face. "It's OK, Shane," she whispered. The knife flashed; Nikki closed her eyes tight. The ripping sound forced one eye open to see Shane cut the sleeve off the coat and examine Nikki's arm.

"I'm glad you're the one to do it. Thanks for trying to save me." Nikki cried and shut her eyes tight again.

"Hey, Nik, um, I think I broke your arm." Shane half-laughed, half-cried.

"What? I'm not bit?" Relief washed over Nikki. The pain throbbed again. Through gritted teeth, she added, "You broke my arm! It is so totally Nikki!" Her pain-blurred eyes looked up into the tearstained face of her friend, who immediately pulled her into a painful hug. "Ow! Ow-ow, you big dork." Nikki laughed and cried into his shoulder.

Hayley and Ray helped her to a seat and fashioned a sling for her. Alistair assured her that Rebecca would be able to set it once they were home.

Introductions were made and stories were told. Krissy and Kyle were playing with Dude with some of the torn fabric from Nikki's coat. The young boy edged forward to play with the cat. Krissy smiled at him. He gave a weak smile back.

"This is Sparky the cat, even though my silly brother calls him Dude Cat. My name is Krissy. What's yours?"

Hayley leaned forward to explain that the boy didn't speak when he croaked, "Brian...can I play with Sparky?"

Home

Alistair put his arm around Rebecca as they opened the high window to the spring breeze. He looked out over the courtyard and smiled. Krissy and Brian played king of the mountain on the rusty overgrown car as Sparky Dude Cat ran after some field mice. Mary and Kyle were sitting in a dark corner of the courtyard, playing with a deck of tarot cards and occasionally laughing.

Nikki walked past and waved at the couple. Mary called her over, asking if she wanted a reading. "No thanks; I have an appointment." Nikki laughed and walked into the front entrance. She met Chris sitting at the bottom of the stairs. She saw Ray and Jen in the large living room, trying to figure out a video game where they had to shoot zombies. Nikki held out her hand; Chris took it. Together they walked up to the watchtower. Opening the door, Nikki saw Shane and Hayley spring apart, both looking rather embarrassed.

Nikki smiled at Hayley, who returned the smile. "How's our friend doing?" Nikki asked Shane. Shane punched up the camera. The lone zombie wandered back and forth by the fallen log. He followed a small path he had worn into the forest floor.

"He seems to be doing OK." Shane smiled as he followed Hayley down the stairs. Nikki smiled at Chris as the door closed.

"Hey, Nik." Chris smiled as he approached her.

"She prefers Nikki." Shane's muffled voice could be heard from behind the door.

Nikki laughed as Chris wrapped his arms around her.